It was no surprise when word came from the home office to send him up to New York, but his entry into the Majors was a big surprise. When he arrived, he was given a locker, a uniform and told to be on the field the following morning. When he called home and told his folks that he was now in a Yankee uniform, they were elated and wished him well. They looked forward to seeing him as soon as he could break away and come home to visit.

He continued to strike out batter after batter and soon the game was over. He had performed the remarkable feat of striking out 27 men with exactly 81 pitches. As he came in from the pitcher's mound, his teammates crowded around him and there was a tumultuous ovation from the stands as a new hero was born. Approaching the dugout, he saw Joe DePlano coming toward him, shaking his hand and embracing him saying, "Tom, that was quite a performance, one that I never thought I'd see and one that I shall never forget. Come on, I have to bring you upstairs. They want to see you."

"OK, I'll go change and we can go right up."

"No, Son. Don't change. They want to see you in your uniform."

"Let's go then."

When they entered the box, Mr. Jameson, the vice-president, came over to them and said, "Hello, Tom, that was quite a performance you gave, one that I am sure will be talked about all over this town tonight and one that will long be remembered. Come, there are some people here that want to see you." With that he brought them over to Skip and Moira, his sister Dr. Alicia Porter Wells, resplendent in her Naval uniform, and to Elvira, her husband Greg and her two children. After kissing and hugging all of them, he introduced Joe DePlano, his coach, to the group. Then looking at all the beaming faces, he remarked, "You know what I see? One happy family." The Wells' family is happily united again.

CHAPTER 1

TWENTY YEARS EARLIER

AS HE OPENED THE door he heard the phone ringing. Dropping his bags, he hurried to the table and picked up the phone.

"Hello!"

"Is that you, John? Where have you been? I've been trying to reach you all week."

"Yeah, well I was upstate fishing. Had to get away and clear my head."

"I know it was pretty rough on you, losing your job and then going through the divorce, but you have to put it all behind you and snap out of it."

"Well, that's easier said than done, but you're right. I have to get my act together and get back in the groove. What's up?"

"John, I've lined up a nice position for you. I know what you're going to say. You're not ready to get back to work, but listen to me. This is a great opportunity and I would hate to see you miss it."

"I don't know if I am ready for anything yet. Rick, you know the divorce left me pretty well shaken."

"John, if I didn't think this was right for you, I would not have called."

"O.K. What's the deal?"

"It's a little company in New Jersey and they need a president."

"Whoa, I am not ready for anything like that."

"Yes, you are and it will be the best medicine in the world for you. In spite of how you feel, you're the man for this position and I wouldn't let it go by."

"Why do they need a president? Isn't there anyone in their organization presently capable of filling his shoes?"

"I don't know. I am only a head hunter and when the request came in, I thought of you."

"What happened to the president? Did he die?"

"No. As I understand it, the parent company was totally dissatisfied with his performance and tried to get him to leave, but he wouldn't go, so they sent a vice president from the home office in California specifically to fire him. Apparently the V.P. took a plane from California, showed up in his office, told him he was fired, and turned right around and went back to L.A."

"Geez, that's pretty rough stuff."

"Well, I guess they had their reasons."

"How am I supposed to hook up with the new people?"

"Well, the principals are here in New York for a few more days, so I am going to arrange for you to meet them at 10:00 AM tomorrow at the Union League in New York."

"The Union League? Rick, this is out of my class."

"Don't worry. These are nice people. They're British and they're looking for someone to run one of their divisions. They know about you, so you have nothing to worry about. Their names are Sir Charles Grayson, Sir William Talbot, and Mr. Robert Hastings. Be calm. Tell them a little about yourself but not too much detail and remember, they're only here to hire a new head-man to run one of their divisions. That man is you! Call me after the interview and we can set up dinner and you can tell me all about it."

After he hung up, John Wells sat down to collect his wits and sort things out, but first he had to fix himself a drink. He was a fairly good-looking man of medium height and build with the trim figure of a golfer. He had dark blond hair and brown eyes and his warm smile told you he was a friendly person. He had been a vice-president with a steel-manufacturing firm, but since his ideas did not mesh with those of his superiors by mutual agreement, he was let go.

His marriage was almost a rocky one from the start. Moira, his wife, had particular ideas about where he should be in his job and constantly nagged and badgered him until one night, after a particularly brutal argument, he made a big mistake and taking some things, he left home. Unfortunately, while he thought that after counseling they could patch things up and get back together again, Moira was not so inclined. The split, when it came, was far from amicable. Moira wound up with the lion's share of the estate and a very hefty alimony settlement that she claimed she needed to maintain the life style she had become accustomed to. This left him devastated and in his despair, he agreed to far more than he should have.

But soon he had to get off the proverbial pot and think of the future. This position, if he got it, could be a godsend. He had some good ideas and had a feel for what should be done and what should not be done. Then he thought, *I should have asked Rick what they manufacture. But no matter. I'll find out tomorrow. First I have to fix me a drink.* Going to the refrigerator he took out a beer. Then putting his things away in the closet, he went into the bedroom and lay on the bed. *President of a company? I hadn't expected any job like that, but I can handle it. For one thing, it will give me a chance to put into practice some of things I have always felt.*

CHAPTER 2

AS HE HURRIED ALONG from Grand Central Terminal, he could not help noticing the large number of people also moving about at this time of the day. No wonder this was such a great city. Arriving at 39th Street, his destination, he saw it was a large four-story building that occupied almost half the block. The exterior was all granite and there at the top in raised letters a foot high were the words UNION LEAGUE.

Climbing the four wide steps, he opened a highly polished brass door and entered the building. The area he entered was a large reception room filled with several groupings of furniture. At the far end and slightly off to the right was a marble counter behind which stood two people engaged in business activities and ostensibly there to serve the needs of the occupants and guests.

Off to the left was a bank of elevators flanked by a marble staircase on the right side. A short distance from the front entrance also on the left side, was an alcove in which a uniformed concierge sat behind a large desk located in the center.

As he entered the concierge rose and asked, "May I help you, Sir?"

"Yes," replied John. "I have an appointment to meet three gentlemen here at 10:00."

"What are their names?"

"Sir Charles Grayson, Sir William Talbout, and a Mr. Robert Hastings."

"And your name, Sir?"

"John Wells."

"Ah, yes, I believe they have already inquired about you. If you follow me, I will take you to them."

Proceeding up the staircase to a mezzanine level, they entered a lounge through a pair of paneled double doors. Walking over to three men sitting before a large fireplace, he said, "Your Lordships, Mr. Wells."

"Thank you, Jameson," said Sir Charles. "Jameson, would you please bring us a spot of tea?" Then turning to Wells he asked, "What would you like?"

"Tea will be fine, your Lordship."

"Please sit down, Mr. Wells. Tell us a little about yourself," asked Mr. Hastings.

"Well, I was born and raised in a little town north of here. I left to go to college in up state New York. After college I knocked around for a couple of years working for several companies in various capacities until I hooked up with the steel company where I moved up to a vice president's position."

"With such a prominent position, why did you leave?"

"My superiors were very conservative people and we had divergent opinions on management practices and directives. I wasn't too happy in the direction we were heading. This lead to many disagreements and realizing that nothing would change, I decided to leave."

"Did you leave because of the disagreements or were you asked to leave?"

"Well, partially because of the disagreement, but I had been thinking of leaving for quite some time and finally made up my mind to go. So by mutual agreement I resigned my position and we parted amicably."

"Mr. Wells, don't you think that when you take a position with a company you owe them some loyalty?"

"Loyalty had nothing to do with it. It was just that some of the more conservative people, who came up through the ranks, resisted any changes. It was difficult for them to accept new ways and methods. They were happy in what and how we were producing our products and resisted any changes in spite of evidence to the contrary."

"Well, you know, Mr. Wells, that is what made some companies great."

"I realize that, Sir, but companies must keep up with the times. They can't remain stagnant. To maintain their leadership they must exploit new ways and technologies to stay abreast of the competition. They owe it not only to themselves, but also to their employees who after all depend on them. I don't mean to sound like a world-beater, but I think companies have to constantly strive to improve their products and eliminate the waste and inefficiency in their operations wherever these crop up. Sometimes this means taking risks. You know, some of the giant corporations in this country are losing ground steadily to foreign enterprises and it's not just because of lower labor rates."

"Very interesting. Tell me Mr. Wells, what do you know about printing and laminating?"

"Well, Sir, when I was younger, for several summers I worked for a local printer in our town who published a local paper and some books. I still have the smell of printing inks and solvents coursing through my veins."

"That's good, Mr. Wells, because one of our divisions over in New Jersey needs someone to take over the helm and quite possibly you might be that man. If we decide that you are that person, what would be your modus operandi and your goals?"

"First I would look over what they have, then see what changes if any should be made toward increasing business prospects. This may mean introducing new products and entering new markets."

"And how would you do that, Mr. Wells?"

"I don't know that yet and I won't know until I see their facilities and operation. How much business is this division doing now? What are their present prospects and goals?"

"About $20 million, but we feel with the right man it has the potential to do much more. Unfortunately, the chap who was in the position we are now trying to fill, had other thoughts with which we were not in agreement. We do feel, however, that whomever we engage should have the latitude to run his own show without our interference. We have interviewed two other chaps, but have not made any decisions yet. Thank you for coming, Mr. Wells. My partners and I will discuss this further and get in touch with you regarding our decision."

Taking his leave from their lordships, John Wells left. He also had some thinking to do. They had opened him up like a sardine can, but he hadn't learned very much about them. This sounded like a good opportunity for him providing they left him alone, as they indicated, to run his own show. Perhaps Rick would know more about them and their operation. He was elated. Of course, he wasn't sure, but he had a feeling as he left that he had the job. If he landed this job, Moira, his ex, was sure going to be surprised. Her motto was *'You go along to get along.'* She couldn't understand why he was unhappy at Howerton Steel, worse why he even left; after all, he was a vice-president.

***

After Wells left, their Lordships and Mr. Hastings had a serious discussion regarding Wells and the other two candidates they had interviewed. It was a lively conversation with pros and cons. Surprisingly each had a different opinion about each candidate.

Finally Sir Charles said, "Gentlemen, there is no doubt that each of the prospects we interviewed is qualified, but in my opinion, Mr. Wells is our man. I detect an aggressive instinct in him and a take-charge attitude that I did not see in the others. With him in charge, I would wager that it would not be too long before we see an increase in business. If you all agree, I think we should call Mr. Richards and tell him Mr. Wells is our choice and then follow with a letter after we return home." All nodded their assent and left it to Mr. Hastings to make the call.

Having concluded their business in New York all that was left was to have Jameson have someone bring down their bags and arrange for transportation to take them to the airport so they could continue on their journey.

PLANE CRASH KILLS THREE

Charleston, SC – Police identified the bodies of three men killed in a plane crash at approximately 3:40 PM Friday as Charles Grayson, William Talbout, and Gregory Norman, the pilot. Another passenger, Robert Hastings, was critically injured and taken to Hot Springs Medical Center in a coma.

The Learjet was traveling from New York's LaGuardia Airport to Charleston International Airport. According to witnesses, the plane appeared to have engine trouble when it hit a high tension power line and burst into flames.

Rescuers recovered the badly burned bodies of the pilot and passengers.

CHAPTER 3

DUSK WAS JUST SETTLING when Ken Fowler entered the Watering Hole. The Hole, as it was called, was a busy neighborhood bar styled somewhat after an English pub. The owner, Mark Leslie, had spent considerable time in Britain after the Second World War. Upon his return to the States, he had opened the pub with the large sum he had amassed through gambling winnings and other sources while overseas. Rising to the rank of staff sergeant, he was one of a small group who stayed on after the war to help dismantle America's war machinery. He was a smart lad who knew how to keep his eyes and ears open and his mouth shut and so always managed to finagle a few extra bucks.

The pub was a large place. It had a rectangular bar in the center with a raised island in the middle on which an organist played a Hammond organ nightly. At the rear of the bar was a small dance floor surrounded by a few tables and a jukebox.

To the left of the bar were two shuffleboard tables which were almost always busy. Off to the right was a row of booths for those patrons seeking more intimacy and privacy.

Sitting in one of the booths was David Fulham, former president of American Laminating Company, nursing a Heineken. Fulham was a tall lean man in his early forties. He had black hair, dark eyes, and a flashing smile that charmed all he spoke to. Some twenty years earlier in his career he had started as a salesman with the American Wrapping Paper Co., a small mom and pop business that produced holiday wrapping paper and ribbons. When the company was acquired ten years ago by British Enterprises Limited and the name changed to American Laminating Co., he became its president. Married with two children, a boy and a girl both in Ivy League colleges, he thought his career was pretty well set until his recent dismissal. As he sat there waiting for several former employees to join him, thinking of how he would bring them on board in this new scheme he had, he thought about his wife Margaret. She had not taken kindly to the news of his dismissal and last evening ended in a big row.

Ken, spying Dave sitting in the booth, walked over and sat down in the booth opposite him. “Hi Dave! How are you doing?” he asked as he sat down.

“Oh, Ken! I didn’t see you come in. Glad you could make it. What are you drinking?”

“I’ll have a Heineken.”

Motioning to the server Dave ordered and said, “What’s the scuttlebutt on my leaving?”

“Well, rumors are flying all over the plant, but no one knows anything.” Ken was the maintenance manager having joined the company when the new company was formed. Of medium build he was in his forties. He had reddish blond hair and blue eyes and was missing a couple of fingers on his left hand as a result of a previous accident with some machinery earlier in his career. He was a good and a fair man who knew his business and machinery. He had started with the company as a maintenance mechanic and had moved up to supervisor in a few years. He had a drinking problem but this did not keep him from running the plant smoothly. Divorced, he had one son in the Marines. "As he sat down he said, "Jesus, Dave! What happened?"

"BEL called in my chips."

"But why? Companies don't normally let presidents go."

"They seemed to feel I was not doing the job they expected. I seem to think there was more to it than that but they were not letting on why."

"I know we were having some problems at the plant, but I didn't feel anything warranted your removal. I thought you had a pretty good handle on the business."

"Though they didn't say so, I think I know what was behind it. There was something going on that no one knew anything about, but let's wait until Jess gets here and then I'll tell you both about it. Speak of the devil, here's Jess. Jess, have a seat."

Jess Chapman was the production supervisor at American Laminating Co. He was a big man in his early fifties and had gray hair and brown eyes. He wore glasses and was well liked by all his men. By nature a hard worker, he was always prepared at any of the meetings. He was a master at scheduling and always made sure that the materials needed for the product they were running was on hand.

"Hello Dave. It's good to see you. I sure was surprised at your leaving."

"Yeah, I guess everyone was, including me. What'll you have to drink?"

"I'd like a gin and tonic." After his drink arrived, he took a sip and said, "I suppose Ken has already asked you the big question."

"Yes, he has and I told him I would hold up until you arrived. Well, nobody knew this, but I was working on a deal to buy the company from BEL. I had heard that some members of the board wanted us out because they felt we did not fit in the BEL family mix of corporations. Somehow Their Lordships Sir Charles and Sir William found out about it and decided to nip the plot in the bud. Since they control most of the companies and most of the money, they decided to get rid of me and replace the two directors. All my talking fell on deaf ears and now, as the saying goes, you know the rest of the story."

"Gee, I am sorry to hear that, Dave," said Ken, "but how did you plan to buy out the company. Do you have that kind of money?"

"No, of course not. What I had planned to do was first borrow a large sum against my house to cover binding the agreement, then float a stock issue to pay down a good portion, and finally pay off the rest with notes from the company's earnings. I figured with some of the board members dissenting, the rest of the members of the board might be in agreement and inclined to accept a deal pressuring Sir Charles and Sir William to sell."

"Where do we fit in?" asked Jess.

"Oh, that's a 64 dollar question. What do you think would happen if the company started to lose business? They wouldn't be too happy, right?"

"Of course not, but I don't see how that affects me."

"Jess, you're a clever guy. As head of production, I think you can figure out how to lose business. Some foul-ups in the production department, a few late deliveries, orders shipped to the wrong customers. Any number of things. I am sure you can figure something out."

"Wait a minute Dave," replied Jess very irritated. "Are you suggesting that I purposely do things to lose business for the company? Why that's dishonest. I won't take the company's money and then knife them in the back. I couldn't live with myself if I did something like that. I couldn't even face my family. You know I always tell my children to be honest and truthful. I couldn't do otherwise. No, if that's what you had in mind for me, include me out."

"Calm down, Jess. This is just business, and it's done every day."

"Maybe so, but I don't subscribe to that kind of thinking. I like to live with myself."

"What have you got against being richer than you are now?"

"Nothing, but if that's what it takes, then I'm not interested. I don't need to live in a bigger house or in a fancier neighborhood or even to own a new and more expensive car. Truly, I'm happy with what I have. I'm not one for the fast shuffle. I believe in giving everyone an honest shake and if it's my lot is to become rich, it will be done through good fortune and my honest efforts."

"Well, I am sorry to hear you say that you're not interested. I figured if we could swing this deal, it could be a sweet three-way partnership. I have some ideas on how we can rebuild the business bigger than it is."

"Dave, I don't think that is the way to go. You know my father was a carpenter, a small man only 5'3", but I saw that man work twelve to fourteen hours a day all through the Depression just to put bread on the table for us. Sometimes I wondered how he managed to carry his heavy tool box around, which I am sure weighed over one hundred pounds, and if I learned nothing else from him, I learned a man's word is his bond and an honest handshake is better than any contract. No, Dave, I prefer to walk down the street with my head held up high and not have to look back over my shoulder."

Dave, a little at a loss for words, finally turned to Ken saying, "How about you? Do you feel the same as Jess?"

"Sort of. I don't know what I could do to affect production."

"You are maintenance supervisor. If machinery doesn't run right, it produces waste and production falls off. Who's gonna blame you especially if you're busy and maintenance schedules fall behind and a breakdown occurs. Breakdowns mean shutdowns and shutdowns mean lost business."

"Well, the new man coming in may be a pretty smart guy and become suspicious. Then I'll be on the carpet and maybe even lose my job. I wouldn't like that."

"Yes, you may be right. He may be smart, but how smart can that be? Just think he is a new man coming into a strange plant and a new operation. He is going to have to spend a lot of time familiarizing himself with the organization and its people. He also has to learn about his product line and the operations required to produce it. It will all take time. When breakdowns occur, how's he going to know why? The worst he can do is tell you to tighten up on maintenance. With old machinery, that's iffy, so there's nothing to worry about."

"I don't know, Dave. I don't feel comfortable with that kind of thinking and I don't want to be a part of it."

"Ken, just think, how many chances do you think will come your way to own a piece of your own company? You still want to pass up this chance because of a little squeamishness? Don't be foolish and let this opportunity go by."

"I hear what you are saying, Dave, and I may never get another chance, but I feel like Jess and I can't accept your offer. I am sorry."

"Well, I think you both are foolish, but if that's how you feel, that's it. A man's got to do what a man's got to do."

"Goodbye, Dave. Thanks for the drink. It was nice seeing you again. I wish you lots of luck and hope everything works out for you."

"Yeah, well it will. Take care and thanks to both of you for coming."

After Jess left, Dave remained seated for some time mulling over his thoughts. *How could I have made such a mistake about these two guys? I surely thought they would be interested. You never know about people. The hell with them. I don't need them. I'll try again to see if I can work out a deal with BEL, but if I can't, I am a smart guy and I am sure I can come up with something else. One thing I am sure of is, if I take over American Laminating, these guys will be out.*

CHAPTER 4

WEDNESDAY MORNING AT PRECISELY 10:00 AM John Wells drove into the parking lot of the American Laminating Company. Pulling into one of the empty guest spaces, he parked his car and walked to the front entrance. Opening the glass door, he entered the lobby. Walking to the back of the room to the receptionist who sat behind a light colored marble counter entering data on a computer, he presented his card. "Good morning. My name is John Wells and I would like to see Mrs. Lowe."

"Is she expecting you, Sir?"

"I believe she may be."

Taking the card and dialing a number on the switchboard in front of her, she waited for an answer. Receiving none, she said, "I don't believe she's in her office. I'll have to page her. Again not receiving any response, she said, "Apparently she's not answering her pager. Can I call anyone else to help you?"

"I should think so. What's your name?"

"Ann Nigro."

"Well, Ann, I am your new president and if any vice-president is available, I'll present my credentials to him."

"Oh, I'm sorry, Sir. I didn't know. I'll call Mr.Overman. He is head of finance and he is here."

"Thank you. I guess it's partly my fault. I should have called Mrs. Lowe and alerted her as to when I would be coming."

"I am glad to meet you, Sir. I'll call Mr.Overman." Again she dialed a number. When he answered, she replied, "Mr. Overman, Mr. Wells, the new president is here and I can't raise Mrs. Lowe. Could you...," but before she could finish her sentence he replied.

"Thank you, Ann. I'll be right down."

While he was waiting, he looked around the room. It had a high ceiling and floor to ceiling windows. Off to one side was a carpeted area which had several arm chairs and tables which were covered with product literature. To say the least, he was impressed with what he saw.

Within a few minutes, a heavy set gray haired man opened a door into the lobby. Walking over to John, he extended his hand and said, "I'm Glen Overman. Welcome to the company. Sorry I didn't know you were coming."

"As I explained to this young lady, I guess I should have alerted Mrs. Lowe as to when I would be coming, but no matter here I am and we can take it from there."

"Yes, well let's go up to my office where we can chat awhile. Then I'll introduce you around if that's ok with you."

"That will be fine."

Leaving the lobby through the door from which Glen had previously entered, they proceeded up a staircase to a hallway on the second floor. Moving down the hallway to the third door on the right side, they entered Glen's spacious, well-appointed office. In the center stood a large, light-colored teak desk on which sat a computer monitor. The desk had several stacks of papers on it. Sunshine streamed into the room from a window behind the desk. Placed against the hallway wall was a leather-covered sofa that had an armchair placed angled to it. At the far end there were also two file cabinets and a console table on which was stacked several large computer printouts against the right wall.

Pointing to the armchair he said, "Please sit down, Mr. Wells."

"Before you go any further, let's drop the formality. Please call me Skip. I don't know where the nickname came from, but from wherever it did, it has stayed with me ever since and I find using it less disarming."

"OK. Then Skip, would you like some coffee?"

"No thank you. Let's just sit and talk. How long have you been with the company, Glen?"

Glen was a man in his late forties and walked with a slight limp. He wore glasses and looked every bit like an accountant. "Almost eight years now. I came here from a large pharmaceutical company that was quite a distance from my home. I live in a town west of here so it's convenient driving here to work. Of course, when I first came, the company was lots smaller but has grown since. How about you, Skip? Where are you from?"

"Clermont. It's a small town in upstate New York south of Troy. Ever hear of it?"

"Can't say that I have."

"It's a small town where you know everybody and everyone knows you. My father was the only doctor in town so we knew everybody. I left to go to college where I earned a degree in engineering. I knocked around for a couple of years in some small jobs and then hooked up with a steel company and now, of course, here I am. I know this is a far cry from the production of steel, but no doubt there probably are some similarities between both operations."

"This is a small company, as companies go, but we do about $20 million a year. We have two big plants in which we produce laminated film and foil products, vinyl, and a type of matting that's used in the manufacture of battery casings. Some of our productions is done in this building but mainly in the one across the street. Why don't I take you around and show you our operation."

"That would be fine, but first if you will show me my digs, I'd like to settle in. How about we put that off until later?"

"Sure thing. Your office is right down the hallway. Come on. I'll take you there."

Leaving the office, they proceeded down the hallway past several doors on both the left and right sides to about one third of the way. Entering a doorway at the right, they saw a woman seated at a desk typing furiously on a computer. She was seated with her right side toward them, so engrossed, she did not see them enter until Mr. Overman said, "Rose, this is Mr. Wells, our new president. Skip, this is your secretary, Miss Rose Shirley."

Rose, stopping what she was doing, came around to the front of her desk and extending her hand said, "How do you do, Mr. Wells. I am pleased to meet you. I apologize for not preparing your office, but no one told me about your coming today."

"That's quite alright. It's really my fault. I should have told Mrs. Lowe when I planned to be here. Please call me Skip." Then looking off to his right said, "If that's my office, then I'd like to go down and get my things and settle in. Glen, how's about, after I finish here, Rose can call you and we can take our tour?"

"Fine. I'll await her call."

Returning in about ten minutes with an attache case, Skip went directly into his office. The office was much larger than

Glen's and was also well appointed with a large dark mahogany desk and two sofas. One against the hallway wall had matching end tables with lamps at each end. The other was against the right wall and had a coffee table in front of it. Against the left wall were two armchairs separated by a table between them. Behind the desk was also a large window. On the left wall there was also a clothes closet and a private bathroom with a square glass enclosed shower stall. The entire room was paneled in a dark wood and was tastefully decorated with pictures and other artwork.

When he finally finished, he called in his secretary. "Miss Shirley, I abhor formalities, so if you have no objections, I prefer to call you Rose and you can call me Skip if that's ok with you. Tell me a little about yourself. How long have you been with the company? Do you live nearby, too?"

Rose was a slim, shapely girl of medium height. She had light brown hair and green eyes and was very tastefully dressed with a skirt, blouse, and blazer. "I have only been here two years. I live not too far from here so commuting is easy. Before coming here, I worked several years as a secretary in an engineering firm. Yes, Sir. I see nothing wrong with calling me Rose except that when you have visitors; then I think I should call you Mr. Wells."

"Fine. In the coming weeks we will get to know each other much better and you will become familiar with what I expect, but for now, my first order of business is to meet my staff. So will you please make the necessary arrangements for a meeting this coming Monday morning at 9:00 AM? I want all the vice-presidents, sales people, and department heads to be there. In addition, please order coffee, buns, pastries and whatever for the group. Then please get out a memo to all the department heads informing them that as of now I have officially taken charge of all company activity. Lastly please call Glen and tell him I am ready for the twenty-five cent tour."

"Before you go, Skip, I think I should tell you that the reason Mrs. Lowe is not here is because she is attending a conference downtown in the mayor's office."

"Oh, what is that about?"

"I think it has something to do with the environment."

"Thanks for telling me, Rose."

Leaving the office, he met Glen and they proceeded down to the manufacturing areas for their tour. The plant was a three building complex consisting of one large single story structure which housed all the big laminators, slitters and traverse winding equipment. It also contained areas for raw materials and finished goods storage.

The other two buildings were four story mill type units located adjacent to each other to form an L. These buildings housed smaller process machinery, the shipping facility, and the entire office staff. The third and fourth floors were occupied by the engineering and the research and development sections respectively. While this complex was not as large as his previous employer's, still what Skip saw impressed him.

Upon their return Glen introduced him to the office and sales staffs.

CHAPTER 5

IT WAS A BRIGHT and sunny Monday morning. The conference room was filled with people drinking coffee and eating pastries and cake from the trays placed on the long, dark, polished table. Some were seated around the table; others were standing and chatting in small groups. The air was filled with excitement. The main thrust was what's the new guy like. Rose had been bombarded all morning with questions, most of which she could not answer. Since his arrival Skip had spent most of his time pouring over computer printouts and although he had been around since the middle of the week, Rose had seen very little of him.

At 8:55 he entered and walking to the head of the table, he deposited his papers. Then spying the pastries, he said, "Um! These look good!" Selecting one, he turned around when he saw Glen.

"Coffee, Skip?"

"Yes, please. Light with milk but no sugar. Unfortunately, I am a borderline diabetic. I really shouldn't be eating this, but what the heck, they look too good to pass up." Moving over to the head of the table, he said, "Good morning, everyone! Rose, is everyone I asked for here?"

"Yes, Mr. Wells."

"Good. Everyone please take a seat. Now we can start. As some of you already know, my name is John Wells, but I prefer to be called Skip. Since my coming Wednesday I have met some of you and looked over your facilities and operations. I have also studied printouts of the business to see how healthy you are. So far things look pretty good. To dispel some curiosity, let me tell you a little about myself. I came from a steel mill where our products were sheet steel, beam sections, re-bar and merchant bar. Though a steel mill is a much different operation than yours, still there are some similarities though remote. In the coming weeks I plan to spend a good deal of my time familiarizing myself better with your product line and operation. I shall also visit with each of you to see what you do and how you do it. If I am going to run this company intelligently, I have to know what its strengths and weaknesses are.

"One thing I do know is that a company is no better than its people. By that I mean that it is the effort, diligence and loyalty that the employees put into it that make a company successful. I may run this company well, but it's you and your people that earn the profit the company makes. Yes, we do have an obligation to the investors, but we also owe something to ourselves. Last year this company earned almost twenty million dollars that is quite a sum. This year I hope we can do much better. To do so, we shall strive to develop new products, reduce our waste, cut inefficiency and improve our machinery. By working together, we shall thus be able achieve the goals we set which in the end will benefit all of us.

"Here are my propositions. To the sales people I say you are our eyes out in the production world. You attend trade shows and see products that our competitors and others make. Perhaps we can produce them, too, thus increasing our product line.

"To you, Bob," looking over to Bob Chester, head of the research department, "I want you to undertake a research program that will yield new products or possibly new and better methods of manufacturing what we now produce. Perhaps you already have some in mind. Let's take a look at them. Remember, if we don't develop new products today, we may have nothing to sell tomorrow.

"Jess, I want you to take a hard look at what we now produce. How can we improve our operation to increase efficiently and lower our waste to reduce our costs?

"Jim, I want you and your engineers to look into upgrading or improving our machinery. Attend trade shows; see how others are doing things. Perhaps we can learn something from them to improve how and what we make. Work closely with maintenance to modify and up-grade our machinery. Better and faster machinery increases our capacity and lowers production costs.

"Ken, we entrust our machinery to you to make it operate smoothly and efficiently and thus hopefully minimizing breakdowns. Breakdowns cause lost productions and eat into our profits.

"Dick, you also have an important part in this equation. If we produce the product, but the order gets fouled up in shipping so that the customer doesn't get his order on time, he is unhappy. Unhappy customers make for bad business. We want only happy customers.

"Mrs. Lowe, I don't know what our policies are for health and retirement. I expect to sit down with you sometime next week and review all of our benefits. Maybe some could stand some improvements."

The meeting continued on for several hours more as questions were raised and answers sought. Finally Skip said, "I think we all have a good handle on what we want to do. My door will always be open to thrash out problems and not let them fester. Thank all of you for coming and I will be visiting with you in the coming weeks."

As Skip left the meeting, he thought - *The words sound good. Now comes the fun to make it happen. Well, I will surely give it my best effort to see that it does.*

CHAPTER 6

DAVE FULHAM WAS NOT one to let grass grow under his feet. Still smarting from the rejections he had received from Jess and Ken, he sat brooding. How had he been so mistaken about those two? Couldn't they foresee the possibilities in what he was offering? Well no matter , the heck with those guys. He would work something out without them. Now he had to think up a plan for he still hoped to take over the company at a much-reduced price. Since he was no longer part of the company, whatever he did had to be done from outside the company. First it would mean doing a little finagling, but nothing that was illegal. After all, it would not do to be successful, but wind up incarcerated.

Then a thought stuck him. If he could take away a good part of the company business and the profits dropped, BEL might be more inclined to accept his offer to buy the company. The first thing he had to do was to go see Charles Beckwith, the president of Southern Wire Company. They were American Laminating's biggest customer buying about 60% of the laminating and slitting production. Hell, they could do their own slitting and he could show them a method commonly used to continuously wrap paper insulation around pipe. It could be adapted to wrapping laminated insulation around the electronic wire they make, thus eliminating buying slitted pads, traverse wound from American Laminating.

Taking up his cell phone, he dialed the phone number of American Laminating's biggest customer. When they answered, he asked for Mr. Charles Beckwith, the president. When he came on the line he said, "Chuck, how are you?"

"OK, Dave. Say, I was sorry to hear about you leaving the company. What the hell happened?"

"Well, politics, but it is long story. Someday I'll tell it to you. Tell you why I called. I am going to be down in your neck of the woods, so I thought maybe we could have dinner together."

"That would be fine, Dave. When?"

"What's a good night for you?"

"I usually have Thursdays free."

"Thursday it is. How about 7:30?"

"That would be OK."

"Alright, I'll set something up. I'll call and let you know where. My regards to Mrs. B and I'll see you then. Take care."

After hanging up, he thought so far so good. *Somehow I'll have to steer him into thinking that they should do their own slitting and traverse winding. Why not? It certainly would reduce their costs. But I'll have to be very careful so that he doesn't smell a rat. I also have to work up a cover story as to why I was in the area.*

Thursday was a nice warm spring day. Dave had driven up the night before and checked into a Hampton Inn motel. Inquiring around, he found the Greenleaf Inn to be one of the better restaurants. Calling ahead, he made reservations for that evening. Then placing another call, when Charles Beckwith came on the line, he said, "Hello, Chuck. How's about I pick you up at 6:00? We can shoot the breeze a bit and then head out to dinner at the Greenleaf."

"That will be fine, Dave. I'll see you then."

***

"Hi, Jess. Got a minute? Maybe I shouldn't bother you. You seem very busy."

"No, it's alright, Ken. I was just working out the schedules for next week. Come in and sit. What's up?"

"What did you think of Skip's speech Monday?"

"I thought it was pretty good. Skip seemed to have a pretty good handle on what he wanted us to do. You know, when Dave came he gave us no directions at all. As a matter of fact, all the time he was here, he never seemed interested much in anything but making sure our bottom line numbers were always in the black. No, I liked Dave. I thought he was a nice guy, but I always had the feeling that he was more interested in his golf game than business. I also know that he put the kibosh on a lot of stuff Bob developed."

"Yes, but you have to admit that business did increase while he was here."

"Yeah, but not because of him. Our business grew because of the increased business from our customers. They bought more. Remember 60% of our production alone went to Southern Wire. Dave always said as they grew, we'd grow. No, I think Skip is more aggressive than Dave and will pay more attention to business than Dave ever did."

"Speaking about Dave, I wonder why they let him go?"

"I don't know, but I think he was wheeling and dealing. Of course, we'll probably never know because no one knows anything."

"What did you think of his offer?"

"Truly, I thought it was insulting. Oh, not that he wanted to bring us in as partners, but what he wanted us to do. That was dishonest. I don't know about you, but I have a sense of loyalty to this company. They have treated me right and put bread and then some on my table all these years and there is no way I'm going to cheat them."

"I felt the same way and told him so. No, I want to go home with my head held up high each day and know that I've earned my keep. But it was a good offer to own a piece of the business. I doubt I will ever get that chance again."

"Yeah, I know, but it's better to look straight ahead than over your shoulder."

***

"Rose, I am going down to the plant. I want to see something, on my way back, I will probably stop by and see Jess."

"OK, Mr. …I mean Skip."

Leaving her, he went downstairs and going across the road he entered the main plant. The plant was a big industrial building with many bays. Some contained rows of pallets filled with polyethylene film, others with aluminum foil, and others with large rolls of laminated material waiting to go to the slitting department. In other bays he saw large process lines where the polyethylene film was coated with a wet adhesive, then dried in a dryer to evaporate the solvent, leaving the adhesive tacky. Then it was combined with aluminum foil and wound into large mill rolls.

Of course, watching this process was not as dramatic as watching steel being rolled, but still it was interesting. One thing he noticed that occasionally an operator would put some adhesive tape on one of the rolls. He wondered why. When he asked an operator, the answer he got was it prevents wrinkles. Not satisfied with the answer, he figured he would ask Jess when he saw him. Walking over to Jess's office which was over in one of the corners of the building, he entered and said, "Hi, Jess. How's it going?"

"OK, Mr. Wells."

"Please call me Skip. What are you doing?"

"OK, Skip. Right now I am preparing work schedules for next week. I prepare the schedules a week in advance for the laminators, slitters, and traverse winders."

"Why?Is there a problem?"

"No, but I have to make sure we have the materials and adhesive we need on hand, schedule the crews and any overtime based on the orders we have. Can't start a run and find out we don't have all the materials or personnel we need."

"Yes, of course. Do you ever have any problems?"

"Not often but there have been a couple of occasions where in a change-over, someone fouled up and not all the materials were here. When that happens, we have to run what we have and then shift over to another product. Of course, that upsets all the schedules and gets everyone annoyed."

" I saw a lot of aluminum baled up in one of the bays. Is that all scrap?"

"Yes."

"What is your percentage of waste?"

"About 17%."

"Wow, that is high. Any serious effort to reduce it?"

"Some. We recycle the aluminum so it's factored into the product cost."

"Is that why I saw all that aluminum baled up?"

"Yes, we generate a lot of waste during startup from wrinkles and any one of a dozen other reasons."

"I saw an operator putting tape on a roll and when I asked him why, he said to prevent wrinkles, but I don't get the connection."

"Well you see, film is extensible, that is it can stretch, but foil cannot not. When the rolls aren't perfectly aligned, the aluminum web forms wrinkles. Putting tape on the one edge the roll helps correct for some misalignment and eliminates forming wrinkles."

"But don't you check the rolls frequently for alignment and make the adjustments necessary?"

"We try and check them at least once a year. For instance to check all the rolls on the number one laminator takes about ten days. To get a shutdown for that long a period was out of the question with our former president Mr. Fulham. He would never allow shutdowns for long periods, so we did partial shutdowns whenever we could and taped the ends of the rolls as a viable alternative."

"That's just plain stupid. I know no one wants to shutdown a production line, but periodically it has to be done."

"I know, but that's how it was. Mr. Fulham was pretty strict on that point and was only concerned with production numbers."

"That's not how it's going to be. I want our machinery to be maintained in tip-top condition.Another thing I noticed – there seems to be a lot of unused equipment lying idle. Any particular reason?"

"Dave, your predecessor, preferred to put most of our effort into the more profitable products so we stopped running some products and the equipment for those lines now lies idle."

"How about those two idle slitters?"

"The slitters we are now running are capable of handling all our production so there's no need to use those two units."

"I see. Well, thanks for the info." With that he left. As he departed, he thought, *I'll have to talk to Bob and see what he can come up with. That waste figure is too high and certainly will have to be reduced considerably.*

As he continued his walk around the plant, hc madc mcntal notes of things he saw somewhat disturbing to him – packing crates lying empty, dollies strewn about and some areas where water had apparently leaked in and caused some damage and as yet had not been repaired. Maybe he was a stickler for neatness, but orderly plants looked better and operated better. He would mention this casually to Jess and those he felt were involved. It wouldn't be a reprimand but a casual word would do.

CHAPTER 7

THE BUILDING FOR SOUTHERN Wire Co. was a big, beautiful building that looked like something out of the Architectural Digest. It had in the past won an architectural prize for its advanced design and beauty. Dave was always impressed whenever he visited the plant. Of course, this time was different. They were no longer his customer. Moving into the lobby he asked for Mr. Beckwith. When he was told to go on down he walked to Beckwith's office.

Arriving there he was greeted by Beckwith himself who said, " Dave, how nice to see you. Come in and sit down. How are you?"

"OK, Chuck. I was coming to this area so I thought I would stop by. You know I am no longer with American Laminating."

"Yes, I heard. You were there a long time, weren't you?"

"Twenty-five years. Started with the original company and became president when BEL took over."

"That is a long time. What happened?"

"There was a bit of dissention back in the home office in Britain. Some of the directors didn't feel that my company should be part of their mix. I was trying to work out a deal with a couple of directors on the board to buy the company. The principal owners found out and thought I betrayed their trust by dealing behind their back, so I was asked to leave."

"Gee, that was too bad."

"Yes it was because what I had in mind would have benefited all of us. But you know some people see things in a different light and you can't reason with them."

"What are you doing now?"

"I am on my own. I formed Atlas Machine Co. and am selling pre-owned machinery. Presently I'm dealing with a customer who wants to buy a printing press." Dave thought, *Since I have to invent a cover story, I'd better make it a good one, especially if I want to reel this fish in.* "How are you guys doing?"

"Not bad but like others we're hurting some. The cable industry is down, especially electronic wiring, because of foreign competition and rising costs. Your former company just raised their prices. All the covering material we put on our wiring and cables we buy from others, so we're at their mercy."

"I know what you mean. When I was president we had to go abroad to buy foil at a decent price. What have you guys done to reduce your costs?"

"The only choice we have to reduce our cost is to improve our efficiency and we've already done that."

"Have your people ever thought of doing your own slitting?" asked Dave.

"No. Why?"

"Well, it could lower your costs considerably."

"None of our people know how to operate a slitter. Besides, I think it would be hard to justify spending a quarter of a million dollars to buy a slitter," responded Beckwith.

"You don't have to spend that kind of money. A good used slitter can be picked up for about forty or fifty grand and it wouldn't be too hard to train your people to operate it especially if you don't want to hire an experienced operator to run it," encouraged Dave.

"But we still would need a traverse winder to prepare the pads we would slit on the slitter into packages we can then feed to the cable winders."

"Not necessarily. You could use the method the pipe people use to wrap pipe which doesn't require traverse wound packages."

"I am not familiar with that kind of equipment. You think we can do it?"

"Oh, yes. I know so. For what you need, you would probably be spending only sixty or seventy thousand dollars at most. It certainly is worth thinking about it. But hey, I didn't come here to talk shop. Let's go eat."

"OK. Do you want me to follow you in my car?"

"No. No, leave it here and I'll bring you back to get it." As they drove off, Dave thought, *Well, I've dangled the bait and I hope it's not going to be too long before this fool seizes it. Things are working out just as I figured. If I work it right, I should be able to clear ten or twenty thousand for myself. Now we'll wait and see what happens.*

***

A week had passed and Dave was home sitting at his dining room table preparing some resumes to give to head hunters when the phone rang. Picking it up he said, "Dave Fulham here."

"Dave, this is Chuck Beckwith. I was thinking about what you said last week about us doing our own slitting. I think it's a good idea. I discussed it with some of my people and they also thought it was a good idea. We think we can do it and are willing to give it a try. Any chance we can we get together and kick it around some?"

"Sure thing. How's about I come down one day next week and we go over it?"

"That will be fine. See you then."

After he hung up Dave thought things were working out great. *Now for the next step. Should I call American Laminating and make an appointment to see the new honcho or just stop in? Just stopping in may look more casual and friendlier, but first I'll have to get some cards made up in a hurry for my Atlas Machine Co.*

***

Walking into the lobby and going up to the desk he said, "Hello, Ann. How are you?"

"Oh hello, Mr. Fulham. How nice to see you."

"Is your new president in and would it be possible to see him?"

"One moment. Let me check."

"Thank you."

Then dialing Rose's extension, she said, "Rose, Mr. Fulham is here and would like to see Mr. Wells."

"OK. Let me check."

"Mr. Wells, our former president is here and would like to see you. Shall I tell him OK?"

"Sure thing, Rose. Send him up."

"Ann, tell Mr. Fulham that Mr. Wells will see him. He says to come on up."

***

Arriving at his old office, he saw Rose. "Hello, Rose. How are you?"

"Mr. Fulham, I am fine, thank you. It's nice to see you. You can go right in. Mr. Wells is expecting you."

Walking into the office, he met Skip coming to meet him. Extending his hand he said, "Hi! I'm Dave Fulham, the previous tenant of this office."

"Yes I know, glad to meet you. I'm Skip Wells. Have a seat. I was sorry to hear about your leaving especially since you were here such a long time."

"Twenty-five years. Hey, that's how it goes. Sometimes heads have to roll and I guess it was my turn."

"I would say we're in the same boat. I had differences with my superiors on my last job and decided it was best to part company. Have you lined up anything yet?"

"No. I have the head hunters looking, but you know it's not easy to place CEOs."

"I imagine not especially in view of the present economic picture, but you never know. Anyhow, I wish you the best of luck."

"Thanks and the same to you in your new slot."

"What brings you here, Dave?"

"Well, while I am waiting to get located, I started my own company, Atlas Machine Co., hoping to sell pre-owned machinery. What got me started was a friend of mine called and asked if I knew where he could pick up a printer. Somebody else I know needs a slitter so I figured, what the heck, let me give it a whirl. The printer I was able to pickup from Phoenix Printed String, but with the slitter I haven't had much luck. Then I remembered you have a couple around here that are idle. So here I am."

"Yes, it seems like we have several pieces of equipment that we're not using including a couple of slitters."

"I know somc people around here didn't agree with me, but the profit margin on the products we ran on some of those machines was so low that I thought it best to discontinue producing them. The machines ran very slow and were labor intensive. The same for the slitters. We upgraded the slitters you are now using in speeds, hydraulics, etc. So there was no need for the other two that are now idle. If you are agreeable, I would like to buy one of the slitters for my client. I think you can part with one and take the money you receive and upgrade the other. In this way you will have a good modernized machine for use as a spare instead to two units in need of work and collecting dust. You know you have a couple of good engineers and an excellent maintenance crew. I am sure they can figure out what's needed and do the work so it shouldn't be too costly."

"You may be right. Let me ask Jess Fowler how he feels. Dialing, Jess he asked, "Jess, you know the two idle slitters we have? Do you think you will ever use them?"

"Not likely. They are too slow and need work. Why?"

"What do you think about selling one and taking the money to fix and upgrade the other? This would give us a good modernized spare."

"Sounds OK to me. Both are just taking up space. Do you have a buyer?"

"Maybe. What would you consider a fair price?"

"I'd say about twenty-five thousand."

"OK. Thanks."

"Well, Dave, it's yours. Do you know which one you want?"

"I think the Dusenberry would be more suitable for what my client wants to do. How about if I give you a check for five thousand to bind our agreement and send the rest when the riggers pick it up?"

"Sounds good. When do you want to pick it up?"

"I don't know yet. How about if I give you a buzz sometime next week after I make all the arrangements and get a rigger?"

"That will be fine."

They continued to chat for the better part of an hour comparing notes on each other's jobs and experiences with Dave telling Skip about some of the products they ran that didn't pan out and his personal observations of some of the staff. Then looking at his watch, he exclaimed, "Holy Moses! Look at the time. Here we sit like a couple of old ladies chewing the fat when I am sure you have many other things to do."

"Oh, that's alright. I enjoyed our conversation. Glad you came. Hope you connect with something real soon. Once again, good luck to you."

With that Dave took his leave thinking, *This poor boob. He's a nice guy. Too bad he's going to get hurt in my plans against his company. That's life. Someone always gets the short end of the stick.*

At the same time Skip was also having some second thoughts about Dave. *He's a cunning bastard. I wonder if the slitter is all he really came for and I don't believe that story he gave me as to why he left. He's a wheeler and dealer. I think he has something up his sleeve. I don't know what, but time will tell.*

***

Picking up the phone again, he called Jess. When Jess answered, he said, "Your former boss, Dave, was here. He bought the slitter."

"He did? What's he going to do with it?"

"I don't know, but I suspect the story he gave me."

"Dave is a pretty smart cookie. I wouldn't trust him."

"I don't. I really would like to know why he bought the slitter. I am sure the story is a much different one than he told me."

"You can bet on it." Then Jess related the incident in the bar about sabotaging the company so that he could put a deal together to buy the company cheaply.

"Thanks for telling me, Jess. I am glad you didn't go along with his suggestion. He seems like a nice guy, but somehow I don't trust him."

CHAPTER 8

DAVE FULHAM WAS STANDING at Lockwod's in the aisle marked Plumbing Supply looking at a rack of copper and plastic pipes when a salesman approached him.

"Can I help you?"

"Maybe. I have a small job to do at home, but I am a bit confused with all these different kinds of pipes. I don't know what to use."

" Well," the salesman said, "the plastic pipe is used primarily for cold water and is easy to install because all you do is cut it to length and glue on the fittings. The bare copper pipe is used for hot and cold applications. It is used mostly by plumbers because a torch is needed to heat and solder on the fittings. The paper covered galvanized pipe is used for cold water when you want to eliminate the pipe from sweating."

" Does the purchaser have to wrap this pipe before he installs it?"

"No, we have a small machine in the back that wraps the paper tape around the pipe."

"The wrapping is so precise, I guess the machine must be pretty complicated."

"Actually, no. It is a very simple machine. Would you like to see it?"

"Oh, I don't want to trouble you, but if you don't mind, I would like to see it. You see I just sold a printer and a slitting machine to a small company and they have an application that's very similar. They wrap paper around several different novelties they make. They're a small mom-and-pop business and if you saw how they now slit rolls to make tape and then the way they wrap their novelties mostly by hand, you'd cry. They're from the old country, but they remind me so much of my parents who died when I was very young that I try to help them whenever I can. By any chance would you have the name of the company you bought the machine from?"

"It's a homemade machine made by a local outfit."

"Do you have the name of the company?"

"I don't have it handy. Why don't you come on back. I'm sure it's on the machine."

"Thanks, I really appreciate this. You don't mind, showing it to me do you?"

"Not at all. Come on back."

Walking to the back of the building, they saw the machine in the corner. Pasted on an upright was a yellow decal which said 'Built by Innovative Machine Works' and gave the address. Dave, looking at the machine said, "It doesn't look like very much."

"Maybe not but it sure does the job. Would you like to see it work?"

"I don't want to put you through any trouble, but yes."

"No problem." Grabbing a piece of pipe and attaching the end of a roll of paper tape to the end of the pipe, he started the machine. In a few seconds the length of pipe was all wrapped.

Astounded, Dave said, "You know I think this is just what they need. Would you mind if I go get my camera from my car and take a couple of pictures?"

"Nah!"

"Thanks. I'll be right back."

Returning, Dave took several shots. The salesman had not taken the wrapped pipe out of the machine so the whole operation was clearly visible. Dave was elated. He had more than he expected. Now he could head to the fabricator, describe what he wanted and get a price. Then next week he could head down to Southern Wire and negotiate a deal for the slitter and winder. Yes, things were looking good he thought.

CHAPTER 9

"HELLO, BOB. HOW'S IT going?"

"Hi, Skip. Come on in and set a spell."

"What are you doing?"

"I'm checking the bond strength of the adhesive on these test strips from laminator #1."

"Why, is there a problem?"

"No, not in these, but there have been at other times."

"Is it because of inconsistency in the formulation?"

"No, it's usually the result of poor drying."

"Oh, why is that?"

"Many reasons. A change in the speed of the laminator, a drop in temperature in the dryer, or a change in air impingement on the web due to clogged nozzles. All serve to lessen the evaporation of solvent from the applied adhesive. Wet adhesive produces a poor bond because the adhesive has not set up."

"How often do you check?"

"We take samples twice each shift. These are some we just took."

"What happens if there's no bond?"

"We have to scrap what we've produced because the laminated material will de-laminate after it is wrapped around the wire or cable."

"Ouch! Is that why I see all that aluminum baled out there?"

"Some yes, but the rest is the normal waste we produce while setting up. Our waste factor is high."

" I heard it's about 17%. Isn't that rather high?"

"Yes, it is and we're working on reducing it."

"I should think so. Have you given any thoughts to the development of any new products?"

Going to his desk, Bob picked up a notebook. "Do you see this book? It's filled with data for new products, but all it has been around here has been an exercise in futility."

"Why for heaven's sake?"

"Because your esteemed predecessor was only interested in running products he deemed the most profitable and he was not inclined to produce low profit items or take any risks."

"Well, that's not very smart. What happens when market conditions change?"

"According to him, you only worry about that when it happens."

"You know he was here in my office a couple of weeks back. He bought the Dusenberry."

"What the hell's he going to do with a slitter?"

"He's in the used machinery business and apparently he had a customer for it."

"There's a guy I wouldn't trust. Did Jess and Ken tell you what he wanted them to do?"

"Yes, Jess did, but I didn't know he also talked to Ken."

"Yeah, that snake. He's up to something. You can bet on it."

"I think you're right. I don't know what it is, but I have a feeling that it has something to do with this company. That's why I would like to get some new products in the mill if possible."

"OK. Let me go through my files again and I'll get with you. We may have to spend some money though on up grading machinery."

"Thanks. I'll look forward to seeing what you come up with."

As Skip left, he thought, S*o I'm not the only one who has reservations about his nibs. I think it might be a good idea to visit some of our customers in the near future.*

***

Three weeks had gone by before Skip could get together with Dick Peterson, vice-president in charge of sales, to call on some of the customers. Today they were calling on Southern Wire Co., their biggest customer. Dick was a big, burly man with red hair and a round face with a large flowing mustache. Originally from Denmark, he had a slight accent. Approaching the receptionist, they asked for Mr. Beckwith and Mr. Ettinger.

"Are they expecting you, Sir?"

"No, but I believe they'll see us. Tell him that Dick Peterson is here with Mr. Wells, the new president of American Laminating and that we are here making a courtesy call."

Dialing Mr. Beckwith, she repeated what Dick Peterson said. When he answered, she pointed to the desk phone. "He's on that line."

"Hello, Chuck. How are you? John Wells and I are making some courtesy calls and stopped by. How about you and Larry joining us for lunch?"

"OK. Let me get Larry and we'll be right there."

Within a few minutes the two appeared and after introductions all around, the four left.

"Chuck, where's a good place to go?" asked Dick.

"At this time of the day I would say the Hunt Club."

"Fine. Hunt Club it is. Why don't you direct us?"

After they were seated in the restaurant, Beckwith turned to John Wells and congratulated him on his new position. Where are you from, John?"

"Call me Skip. Pennsylvania. I was with Howerton Steel."

"That's a far cry from your present company."

"Yes, it is, but you know there are some similarities. Anyhow I find my new company fascinating. But you know, like any new job, no matter what you know, you always learn something new. For instance, we're trying to develop some new products a little different than those we are now running and hope we are successful."

"I wish we could do that. Foreign competition is causing havoc with us and the market for electronic wire and cables is shrinking and we are feeling the effects."

"That's too bad. Don't you have anything else to pickup the slack?"

"We hope our fiber optic business will take up the slack and then some, but only time will tell."

"Is there anything else you can get into?"

"We just bought some new machinery and hope that will make a big difference in our operation."

"I wish you luck."

Of course, at this point neither Wells nor Peterson knew that Southern Wire had bought the Dusenberrry nor what the impact was going to be. This would come later.

They continued chatting away till Dick, looking at his watch said, "Chuck, we have to take off because there's a another call we want to make."

"Of course. Well, it's been nice to meeting you, Skip, and the best to you."

When they drove back to the plant, Larry said, "Would you mind dropping me off at the back of the plant instead of the lobby?"

"No problem. OK if we drop Chuck off first and then take you around to the back?"

"Sure."

After Larry left and entered the plant, Dick drove to the end of the lot to turn around. As he was making his turn, Skip said, "Hold it a minute." Getting out he walked over to a large packing crate and on it saw stenciled *American Laminating, Co.* "Son of a bitch," he said, "They bought our Dusenberry."

"No," remarked Dick. "How do you know that?"

"I recognized that crate because it contained the spare parts and shafts we gave the riggers. But slitting is not going to be any good to them unless they can traverse wind their slitted pads. I expect Dave will now be back to try and buy one of our unused winders."

Mill rolls are large rolls of flexible material wound on a shaft. At American Laminating, mill rolls were 42" diameter x 72" wide rolls of aluminum foil laminated to plastic film. After lamination, the rolls are moved over to a rotary slitting machine which then cuts the rolls into several multiple pads using razors set at customer specified predetermined widths. When finished, the pads are taken from the slitter and placed onto a traverse winding machine. Here they are now wound into more compact spools much like thread is wound on a sewing machine bobbin. The slitted pads produced by the slitter are large in diameter and narrow in width and as such are somewhat unstable. Traverse winding rewinds them into smaller compact packages making them much easier to handle in the next step which is the covering process over wires or cables.

"They don't know that we now know they plan to slit," said Skip. "So expect that anytime soon, they will cut back on their orders to us. But I have news for them, if any of the new products I discussed with Bob take off, which I believe will, we will be able to drop Southern Wire completely as a customer with no loss of income."

"I hope you're right, Skip."

"I hope so too, but from what I have seen of some of the stuff that Bob has developed, your people are going to be busier than they have ever been."

CHAPTER 10

THREE MONTHS HAD PASSED since Dave first visited Southern Wire and sold them the slitter and winder. Now sitting in Chuck Beckwith's office he asked, "How's it going, Chuck? Are your people proficient with slitting and winding now?"

"Yes, they are. They have been practicing slitting paper and doing quite well."

"You know slitting paper is not exactly the same as slitting laminated foil."

"Yes, we know. We bought a couple of rolls of laminated material from Chase Aluminum and the boys did very well with that. As a matter of fact, we now have been cutting back on our orders to American Laminating. You know John Wells and Dick Peterson were down here on a courtesy call some time back."

"Jesus, I hope you didn't tell them you bought a slitter?"

"No, of course not, but I did tell them that we might be cutting back on our orders because of foreign competition and that the market for electronic wire and cable, in general, was shrinking."

"How did they take the news?"

"Not too well although Skip did say they were trying to develop some new products."

"I know what Bob worked on while I was there. What they've got is nothing. That's why I would not allow them to run any of the stuff Bob developed. They were all low profit items or products we didn't want to get into."

"Gee, I am sorry to hear that."

"Oh! Don't worry about them. Feel sorry for Skip because he's a nice guy and he doesn't know that all he has is a bunch of losers working for him. Most are too afraid to take any risks and are happy in their own little worlds. So how can the company grow?"

"What's going to happen to them when they lose our business?"

"They'll probably go back to being a small company again. You know when I first joined them, they were only a mom and pop business. I built them up to what they are now. Good luck to you, Chuck. I am glad things worked out. I'll keep in touch and who knows, I might run into a deal soon you may be interested in."

As he drove away, he thought, *Yes, Siree. Things are working out. I'd like to see their faces when Southern Wire tells them they are only going to buy mill rolls. Another thing, I may be able to get these guys interested when I work my deal with British Enterprises. Yeah, they might just be interested in coming in this deal with me.*

***

Rose was in the middle of taking dictation from Skip when Jess walked in.

"Jess, what's up?"

"I just got word from Larry Ettinger at Southern that they are going to do their own slitting and winding and only want to buy mill rolls from us. When I asked Larry how come, he said they got a good deal on a slitter and winder and decided to do their own. It's part of a move to keep costs down."

"Well, I knew it was coming. I just didn't know when. Beckwith inferred as much to Dick and me when we were down there on a courtesy call. He said that they would be cutting back on their orders. When I asked why, he gave me a cock and bull story of how they were hurting because of foreign competition and a shrinking market. Of course, he doesn't know that we now know they bought our Dusenberry. As we were leaving the plant, we spotted the crate that contained the shafts and spare parts we sold them sitting around the backside of the plant."

"OK, so he bought the slitter, but what about a winder?"

"I would guess he has probably bought that too from someone else."

"What are we going to do now?"

"Nothing we can do except grin and bear it and hope that Bob can come up with something someone needs real soon."

"What shall I do with the operators from the slitters and winders? Let them go?"

"When did he say this was going to happen?"

"He's canceling everything we have except what's presently in progress."

"What does that mean?"

"If we stretch it, to the end of the week at best. Should I let the operators go?"

"No, these people depend on their pay checks each week. Let them take their vacations and when they come back, put them on whatever you can. A company this big should be able to carry some of its employees for a while. Hopefully it won't be too long. Tell them we'll try to make it up to them later on."

"That damn Dave! I never knew he was such a snake," muttered Jess.

***

Almost a month had passed since Southern Wire had cut back their orders. Laminator #1 was still busy, but the slitters and the traverse winders were slow. The time had been put to useful gain. The plant had been cleaned up and painted, needed repairs to machines had been made, and inventory stocks had been reduced to more practical levels. Time hung heavy with uncertainty.

But there was a bright spot. Jim Porter, the chief engineer, had his wife bring in their triplets. At a little over two years of age they were cute as buttons. The two girls were dressed identically with pink dresses and hats, and the boy in a blue sailor suit. Of course, everyone wanted to hold them and fuss over them. Jim Porter was a good-looking heavy-set man thirty-nine years old. This was his second marriage. He had slightly graying hair and wore thick glasses. He and his wife Mary had tried unsuccessfully to have children until finally they opted for in-vitro fertilization. The news that they were going to have triplets was like music to their ears and you could not find a happier couple. Now, of course, as he looked over all the fuss the office gals were making over his youngsters, you couldn't find a prouder father.

Mary, a good-looking tall, buxom woman with light brown hair and brown eyes, was even happier than Jim. At thirty-eight this was her first marriage. She had indicated to Jim that she wanted children and was disappointed when the medical results indicated she was barren. When the subject of invitro fertilization was broached, she jumped at the opportunity. After the fetuses developed and she was told she was carrying three, she refused to eliminate any saying, "How can I kill my babies?"

CHAPTER 11

SKIP WAS SITTING IN his office talking on the phone to one of his friends at Howerton Steel when Dick Peterson walked in.

"Got a minute?"

"Sure thing," answered Skip cutting his conversation with his friend. "I'll call you back later, Fred." Then he hung up.

"What's up, Dick?"

"Hold on to your socks because we just got a tremendous order from Lyden Insulation Co. that's going to keep us busy for the rest of the year."

"That is good news! You know we couldn't have kept our traverse and slitter operators idle much longer. I guess that is a big part of what Bob developed."

"Yes, and they loved the samples he sent them."

"When do they want to start taking delivery?"

"Starting the first of next month."

"That should give Jess plenty of time to order materials and make the changeover."

"Not only that but they also liked the samples we sent them for the vinyl and aluminum duct tapes. As soon as they finish evaluating them, they'll probably cut us some orders for those, too."

"Dick, do you realize what's happening? If any of your boys come back with orders for any of the food wraps Bob came up with too, we're going to be busier around here than the proverbial one-armed paper hanger with the fleas. I guess I'd better get a letter out to Chuck and tell him that as of the first, we will be discontinuing producing mill rolls for him."

"Skip, I'll bet he's going to be surprised and I don't think he's going to be too happy with the advice he got from Dave."

"I know he won't, but that's his problem."

Calling Rose, he dictated the following:

July 17, 1988

Mr. Charles Beckwith, President Southern Wire Co.
Columbia, South Carolina

Dear Mr. Beckwith:

In our pursuit of new business, we are changing our product mix. As a result we no longer will be producing various products we now run. Among these will be mill rolls we now produce for the wire and cable industry. We regret having to do this because we look back over the years for the long and profitable relationship we have had with Southern Wire.

We wish you well and are sure you will find some other manufacturer to accommodate your needs. We will complete all the present orders we now have on hand and as of August 1, but we will not be accepting any new orders for those products. Once again, thank you for your past patronage and we wish you the best.

Sincerely,

John Wells, president

"Rose, you fill in the address and get this right off then arrange a staff meeting for Friday morning at 10:00 AM. Also tell Elizabeth I would like to see her. Thanks."

***

As was Dave's usual custom if not dining at home, whenever he pulled in, he stopped in the kitchen and made himself a cup of coffee. It was nothing fancy - a cup of water placed in the microwave for a few seconds, two spoonfuls of instant coffee and he was set. He had a hard day and had driven many miles. Selling used machinery was not so easy especially when the economy was down as it was now. As he was sipping his coffee and mulling over the day's events, Maria, the housekeeper came in.

"You got a lot of phone calls. Some man's been trying to get you all day. He say it very important you call him no matter when you come home."

"Really? What's his name?"

"Mr. Bootstrap. He leave his number."

"Bootstrap? I don't know anyone by that name."

"I no know nothing. I only know he call many times."

"OK, give me that slip. I'll go call him now." Going into his study, he dialed the number. When a woman answered, he said, "My name is Dave Fulham. I would like to speak to Mr. Bootstrap."

"Oh Dave, this is Laura Beckwith. Charlie wants to talk to you. Charlie, Dave Fulham is on the line."

When Beckwith came to the phone he started with, "Where the hell have you been? I've been trying to get you all day. That damn company of yours is not going to supply us with mill rolls anymore. If they don't, what are we going to do? It means closing the plant. I'm going to have to lay off a lot of people. We won't be able to supply our customers. Oh Jesus! We should never have gotten into something we didn't know anything about and now we've got all kinds of trouble and I don't know what we are going to do. Jesus! What a mess we're in." Like a child with a broken toy, he rambled on incoherently and completely distraught.

"Whoa, whoa! Slow down, Chuck. What are you taking about?"

"Your ex-company told us as of August 1st they are not going to supply us with mill rolls anymore. I don't know what we're going to do. How can we survive?"

"Hold it, Chuck. Who told you that?"

"The president John Wells sent us a letter."

"Chuck, calm down. Listen to me. He's bluffing. You're his biggest customer. If he cuts you off, he's out of business."

"He says he has a bunch of new products."

"Chuck, listen to me. I know what they have. They have nothing new. He's just trying to scare you so that you return to your old status. Believe me, just sit tight for a while and you'll see they'll come around."

"You think so?"

"Chuck, I know so. They have nothing they can run. Remember I was there; I know what they have. Bob Chester is a zero. What he developed you couldn't give away. That's why I wouldn't permit them to run what he developed."

After he finally got Beckwith calmed down, he hung up the phone. Then he started to think. *What's the matter with Skip. Can't he see where his bread is buttered? Well, if he wants to play hardball, we can play that game, too and he'll be the loser. I know the stuff Bob had. It was crap. That's why I wouldn't tie up our machines running any of it.* Then he thought, *I think I'll pay Mr. Wells another friendly call and see what he's up to.*

***

It was Thursday before Dave could get to see Skip. Ostensibly he pretended to see if they had any machinery they wanted to get rid of. He was surprised when Skip told him they were busy and would be for a very long time with some new products Bob had developed. He acted more surprised when Skip causally told him they had dropped Southern Wire and Cable. Not seemingly particularly interested, Dave pointed out that Southern Wire had been a big customer for a long time and was it wise to drop them. When Skip mentioned that they were entering new fields with new products and so far the picture looked very bright, he was surprised and realized that nothing further could be gained. He wished them well and took his leave. Now he thought, *This guy is smarter than I thought, but I think he's bluffing. What could they possibly have that I didn't know about? We shall wait and see. Meanwhile I think I'd better talk to their lordships. Hopefully they've changed their minds and are willing to sell.*

***

Elizabeth Holly was a tall, good-looking woman. She was full figured matronly in appearance with green eyes and dark hair tinged with splashes of gray. Married and divorced, she lived with her two sons, Ian age fourteen and Jason age sixteen. She had been with the company nine years starting in accounting and then moving up to be vice-president when Glen Overman came on as controller. She had a degree in accounting and a Masters in Business Administration. Stepping into Skip's office, a little apprehensively, she inquired, "You wanted to see me, Skip?"

"Yes. Please close the door and have a seat." After she was seated, he said, "As you know I was hired through a head hunter, but what surprised me more than anything else was that no one in this organization was chosen to fill my predecessor's shoes after he left."

"To a certain extent, Dave was a nice guy but not one to do anyone favors. As far as women were concerned, he had a blind eye. He never asked my opinion and the only time that he and I talked was if something pertained to business or in answer to one of his questions," replied Elizabeth. "I would guess, if he were asked, he would not recommend any of us."

"I am surprised because he seemed like a nice guy when he visited here, but after I heard what he wanted Jess and Ken to do, I had doubts." Then he related to her what both had told him. "Let me ask you a question. Are you happy here?"

"Truthfully, no."

"I kind of surmised that. Why?"

"I just told you. Under Dave I was just another fixture here. If I didn't need this job, I would leave."

"You're divorced, aren't you?"

"Yes."

"Any children?"

"Yes, two boys - one fourteen and the other sixteen."

"I don't mean to pry, but where's Mr. Holly?"

"I don't know. He cleaned out our bank accounts and left me with a big credit card debt. He hasn't paid anything toward child support either. Thank God I have my mother with me. She helps me a lot and looks after the kids."

"I guess it has been pretty rough for you."

"Yes, it has."

"I don't want you to leave, Elizabeth. I think this company needs people like you. I want you to be my backup in all respects. As of this moment, you are now our new executive vice-president and that comes with a raise. Congratulations! From here on in you and I will be working closely together."

Elizabeth was so stunned she didn't know what to say. Then with tears in her eyes, she got up and walked over to Skip hugging him and planting a kiss on his cheek. She said, "You wonderful, wonderful man. How can I ever repay you?"

"None needed. Just enjoy the moment. I'll have Rose type out a notice and post it throughout the company. To get back to business, as you know we now are very busy and going to be even more so when we start producing flight insulation for Boeing's 757's and Europe's A-380's. The Environmental Protection Agency has been on our back regarding the solvent fumes we discharge into the atmosphere. Up to now we have been lucky. We've been able to get by on the credits that we've purchased from other companies by using and submitting their unused fume discharges to the atmosphere in our reports to the Environmental Protection Agency. I don't think we can pussyfoot around much longer, so I want you to head up a project to get what we need to be in compliance with the new regulations."

"I am going to need help with this project."

"Yes, I know. Check with Rosemary Lowe to see what she found out at the meeting she attended. From what I gathered, we have to cut our emissions into the atmosphere considerably. This means we have to install an incinerator. We're also going to need a bag-house to filter the exhaust fumes to the incinerator. Besides that, we'll need a new duct system to pick up the exhaust discharge from all the dryers to convey the fumes it to the bag-house. I think we should locate the units on the west side of the plant between the plant and the railroad and relocate the underground solvent tanks now buried there to the front of the building. Get Jim Porter to work out the details and set up specs for all of the equipment and then get the necessary bids. Use Bob, Jess, and Ken as you need them. After you have set up a budget for the project, come in and we'll set up the necessary financing with Glen."

"Skip, I want to thank you for giving me this project. I won't let you down."

"I know you won't, Elizabeth. I have every confidence in you and the rest of my staff. Keep me informed when you're ready. Incidentally, don't thank me because when you're finished, you may curse me!"

CHAPTER 12

IT WAS THE BEGINNING of October when Dave decided this was a good time to talk to Sir Charles. By now he reasoned Sir Charles must be aware that American Laminating had lost considerable business and was scrounging around for new products. He might be more amenable to sell at this time. He was totally unaware of the new changes that had taken place at American Laminating. He remembered the day he talked to Skip some time back and Skip had told him that things were slow as a result of the drop in business from Southern Wire. He still did not believe Skip's new story that they were now very busy with new products. Dialing up the number, when someone answered, he said, "This is David Fulham. May I speak to Sir Charles?"

"I am afraid that is impossible. Sir Charles is dead."

"Good Lord! No! What? When?"

"It was on his last trip to America. He was in an airplane they had chartered and was killed when it crashed."

"With whom am I speaking?"

"Williams, Sir. I am his butler."

"I am sorry; Williams. Do you have the number for Sir William Talbout?"

"I am afraid he's dead too, Sir."

"Oh my God! I almost hesitate to ask how's Mr. Hastings."

"He's dead also. He returned to England in a coma and died about a month after his return. May I ask you, Sir, what is this in reference to?"

Now Dave thought, *I am sorry they're dead, but what luck! With these three guys gone, I may be able to bluff my way into a deal with whomever now is handling their affairs.*

Responding to Williams's question he said, "Sir Charles was considering my proposition to buy American Laminating Co."

"I know nothing about that. Perhaps young Mr. Charles can help you. He is handling all Sir Charles's affairs. Let me call him."

"Thank you. I'll hold."

When the younger Charles came on the phone, he repeated what he told Williams."

"Well, Mr. Fulham, I am unfamiliar with what you're saying. I would suggest that you ring up our solicitor Sir Arthur Clewiston of Clewiston, Clewiston, and Clewiston. Perhaps he can be of some assistance. They are located in Trafalgar Square."

"Thank you. I'll call them now. My condolences to you on the loss of your father."

Of course Dave was sorry to hear that the three principals had died, but now he thought with them gone, nobody would know whether he had a deal or not. *I may just be able to bluff my way into one.*

After asking information for the phone number he needed, he dialed it and asked for Sir Arthur Clewiston. When the solicitor answered, he introduced himself. “My name is David Fulham and I was formally president of American Laminating Co. Sir Charles was considering a proposition I offered to buy the company.”

“I do not recall his ever mentioning that he wanted to dispose of that company.”

“Maybe he hadn’t gotten around to it, but now that that company is doing so poorly, I am sure he probably would have considered it.”

“Poorly did you say?”

“Yes, they lost one of their biggest customers and have had to sell some machinery and lay off people.”

“What you are saying does not agree with the latest information I have. Their last statement shows they are extremely busy … that they are buying new equipment and plan to expand to another building.”

“That can’t be true. Who is the statement from?”

“I believe the statement is from Mr. Overman, the controller, and the letter is from Mr. John Wells.”

“I don’t understand it.”

“Well, Mr. Fulham, I can only relate what I have. If you have a different opinion, I suggest you discuss it with Mr. Wells. I can tell you one thing, with that company doing so well, I am of the opinion that the Board of Directors of British Enterprises, Ltd. will be reluctant to dispose of it at this time.”

“All right, Sir. I will call Mr. Wells. Thank you for your information.” Hanging up the phone, he sat there stunned. How could they be doing so well? He simply could not believe it. He remembered what Bob Chester had been working on. It was junk. What had he now developed that made them so busy? No, something was wrong. They were giving BEL false information. He was sure of it. Then he thought, *I’ll give Skip another call. No, maybe a visit might be better. This way I can see for myself whether or not they're busy. Yes, that's what I'll do.*

***

The next morning at 10:00 Dave was at American Laminating. As he drove up he could see two trailers sitting in the loading bay and two more waiting on the street to get in. Can this be true? It sure looked like they were busy. When Skip told him to come up, he wasted no time getting there. After exchanging the usual pleasantries with Rose, he entered Skip's office.

"Hi, Dave! What brings you here?"

"To find out if you have any machinery for sale and also to see how you guys are doing. You know I have a soft spot in my heart for this company."

"Well thank you, Dave, for your interest. We went through a bad time, but now we are doing very well. We have three shifts going full blast and have taken additional space in the building across the street where we're now installing our new laminator."

Dave was so taken by this new turn of events, that he didn't know what to say, but finally he blurted out, "Gee, that's great. I'm happy for you guys." He could now see that his dream of buying the company cheap was out of the question.

He was brought back to reality when Skip asked, "How are you doing?"

"A little better than I expected, but actually there's not much moving these days. What are you guys running that makes you so busy?"

"Some new products Bob developed. The vapor-insulating barrier that forms an integral part of home insulation and several kinds of duct tape."

"That's great!" But to himself, *Son of a bitch! I never thought we could break into that market. How could I have been so mistaken? Now What? Who the hell is going to sell a company that's doing good? Well, you never know.* Then a thought struck him and he said to Skip, "You know it seems a shame that all this profit you're making is going overseas to BEL especially when they haven't done anything to earn it. Have you ever thought of buying the company from BEL?"

"No, I haven't. Besides, where would I get the money to make it happen?"

"With the three principal owners now dead, young Grayson and the board might be inclined to sell. You know young people today. They're only interested in the high life and not running businesses. Besides, some members of the board previously didn't feel this was the right product mix for their enterprises and might still be inclined to sell."

"You say the principals are dead? When did they die?"

"I really don't know. I believe a few months back when they were here in America. Apparently they chartered a plane and died when it crashed."

"I'm very sorry to hear that, but again I say I don't have the where-withal to swing that kind of deal."

"Don't be too sure. Some loans could be approved to cover a down payment and the major portion required could come from floating a stock issue. It wouldn't be difficult especially in view of the company's past track record, your present business climate, and your future projections."

"Gee, I don't know. I don't think we're ready yet for that big an undertaking."

"I know how you feel, Skip. You just took over the reins of running the company and this would be a giant leap. But believe me, it wouldn't be that hard. I have a couple of friends in a Wall Street brokerage firm who could handle the stock issue."

"I don't know."

"Think about it instead of working for someone else, you'd be working for yourself. How many times do you think you'd have the opportunity to own a big piece of your own company?" Then looking at his watch, he said, "I gotta go, but I'm happy to hear you guys area doing great. Think about what I said and call me if you decide to give it a go."

When he left, Skip leaned back in his chair and thought, *That fox! He didn't come to buy any machinery; he wanted to see how we were doing. Now he knows. His scheme to buy this company cheap is dead! I didn't know that Grayson, Talbout, and Hastings died. I wonder how come no one called. Can it be that no one is really interest in us? Maybe Dave is right. This might be a good time to approach BEL with an offer. I'll have to talk to Liz about this and bring it up during a staff meeting.*

CHAPTER 13

ALMOST A YEAR HAD passed since Skip headed up American Laminating. The company was prospering and things were looking good. A new laminator had been installed and it also was running with three shifts. It was at this point that Bob Chester came to see Skip. Poking his head into the doorway, he asked Rose, "Is he busy?"

"Yes, but I think you can go in."

Stepping into the office he said, "Skip, I just got a call from Chelsea Foods and they want to go ahead based on the samples we sent them two months ago."

"What kind of samples did we send them?" asked Skip.

"Foil printed and laminated to paper."

"Printed foil? We can't print."

"No, we'll only laminate the foil and paper for now and someone else will do the printing until we get our own printer."

"What do they use our product for?"

"Wrapping butter, cheese, margarine, chocolate, and any number of different foods. Apparently foods kept well in the samples we sent to them."

"You know laminating is tight right now. Laminators #1 and #2 are tied up full time with what we're running for Lyden and Boeing."

"I know, but these are narrow widths and we can use the two old laminators we have. We're going to need printers and dryers for each line though."

"That may not be too difficult. Atlas Machinery can probably get us the printers and dryers we need. Are we talking big orders?"

"Initially no, but later on I would say yes."

"When do we start delivering?"

"The middle of next month."

"Next month? There's no way we can buy printers and get them operational that quick."

"I know, but we can do the laminating and sub the printing out until we have our own units operational."

"That's a good idea. Well, tell them OK. Then we'll see about getting the dryers and printers we need. Maybe Dave might have a lead on what we want."

"You're going to call Dave? With so many other machinery dealers out there, he would be the last guy I'd call. I wouldn't even call him to ask for the time of the day."

"Yeah, I guess you're right. It's just that I figured I'd help out a new guy in business."

"After what he wanted to do to us? No way!"

"You're right, Bob. Tell you what. Get with Jess to determine and order the materials we will need. Then you and he get together with Jim and have engineering look around to see where we can pick up the printing and drying equipment we need. Have them contact used equipment dealers first to keep the cost down." As Bob got up to leave, Skip continued, "Bob, thanks for coming through. I appreciate your efforts."

After Bob left, Skip thought *And Dave stifled this guy? Boy was that a mistake! I think he deserves a raise.* With that kind of thinking, he doubted if Dave would have exceeded by much the $20 million they were doing before his arrival.

When Bob left, Skip thought about what Dave had asked him. Picking up the phone he dialed Elizabeth. After she answered, he asked if she could come to his office.

"Be right there, Skip."

When she arrived, he told her to shut the door and have a seat. Once seated, he proceeded to tell her, "You know for sometime now Dave Fulham has been trying to buy the company apparently with little success. When he was here last time he suggested that I think about buying the company."

"Do you have that kind of money?"

"No, of course not, but what he suggested we could do is secure loans to cover the down payment. Then using some friends he has in a Wall Street brokerage firm, have them help us issue stock for the larger amount. Any remaining balance could be paid off by notes against our earnings."

"Can we do that?"

"I think so."

"You know while Dave seemed like a nice guy, no one around here really liked him and I don't think he's changed."

"No, you're right especially after what he wanted Jess and Ken to do."

"That's Dave."

"Well, I think buying the company might be a good idea if it could be arranged. But here's the problem. If Dave's part of the deal, what position will he assume? If he comes back here as president, some employees would be unhappy. Then I would be out and some of the things we now have planned or are doing he may cancel. If I stay on as president, we could continue on as we are now doing, but he would become chairman of the board.

That would make me unhappy having him above me looking over my shoulder."

"Does Dave have to be part of the deal?"

"Well, it was his idea and supposedly he has the brokerage friends who can help us with the stock issue."

"I don't want to malign him, but if you decide to go with him on this deal, count your fingers after you shake his hand."

"As bad as that?"

"Well, I saw him pull some shady deals that I wouldn't be proud of. Do you really need his help?"

"No, I suppose not. I think if I decide to buy, I surely could find a brokerage firm that could handle the stock issue. You know this company has had a very good track record over the years and presently our business outlook looks very promising. There are many small cap companies that wished they looked as good as we do."

"Why do you want to buy the company? Is it really that important to you to own something this big? Do you realize the enormous debt you will incur? In my opinion, you have as much prestige now as president as you will have if you became the owner and certainly not have as many liabilities. I think you should count your blessings."

"You're probably right, Elizabeth. Now that I think of it, I'm sure it's not going to be easy to raise the capital that will be needed. With our present forecasts I know the amount may be considerable. But one thing that bothers me is to have Dave hanging around in the wings to do just that. If he is successful, it will be curtains for several of us."

"I hear what you're saying, Skip. No doubt Dave will try. He might even be successful, but I doubt he will get rid of all of us. What I think you should do is wait him out and see if BEL even considers his proposition, especially since we are doing so well.

I think that before they accept any offer from Dave, they will come back and ask you if you have a counter offer. At that time you can decide if you are still willing to buy the company."

"You know, I'm glad I discussed this with you, Elizabeth. You have steadied my thoughts. You're right. Let's wait out Mr. Fulham."

After Elizabeth left, Skip thought, *This woman really has a good head on her shoulders and I'm glad I chose her for my exec. She will be a good steadying influence for me. I wonder what Dave will do now? Buying the company won't be easy even for him.*

Elizabeth was elated that Skip took her into his confidence, not only that, but he respected her opinion. This was the second time he placed his trust in her – the incinerator project which was proceeding well along and now this. Yes, she was happy. Her intuition told her that somewhere down the road Dave was going to be trouble and she had severe misgivings about it. Time would tell.

CHAPTER 14

AFTER A PARTICULARLY RESTLESS night, Dave Fulham awoke at 7 AM. As was customary, he would lounge in bed for a quarter of an hour or so and then get up, shower, shave, dress, and go downstairs for breakfast. His breakfast usually consisted of two pieces of buttered toast, a glass of orange juice, and a cup of instant coffee. The coffee was made by heating a cup of water in the microwave. Then he added the coffee, a Sweet and Low, and some fat free milk.

He was never a big eater, but when Margaret came down before him, she prepared cereal, stewed prunes or a slice of melon, and two fried eggs with bacon or sausages. When he protested, she'd say, "Nonsense! A grown man has to eat to keep up his strength and breakfast is the most important meal."

However, this particular morning he lay in bed thinking. Skip hadn't gotten back to him about buying the company from BEL. He thought this strange because Skip had been such an upbeat guy. From what he had seen, the company was doing well and their prospects were good. Though dropped by Skip and American Laminating, he had managed to hook up Southern Wire with Chase Laminating who was happy to supply them with all the mill rolls they needed. This finally got Beckwith off his back and he stopped pestering American Laminating.

Even when he discussed it with Margaret, she also thought it strange but disagreed with him as to the reason Skip had not called him. She remembered the stories her parents told her of the Depression years and she was happy with what they had. Though not wealthy, they were living comfortably and enjoyed a fair measure of luxury. She couldn't understand this desire in Dave to reach for the moon, as she called it, and she thought she could well understand Skip's reluctance to assume a big debt. She told Dave, "Listen, why don't you leave that poor man alone? He's in a new job and he has enough on his plate to keep 150 people working. I think he feels that he doesn't need to take on a big liability just to gain more prestige."

Maybe Margaret was right Dave thought. Skip was feeling his way around in a new job and didn't want to assume the additional burden that buying the company would entail. A lot of guys are smart but lack the gumption to take the big risks. Finally rising, he went into the bathroom to shower and shave. Finishing, he dressed and went downstairs to prepare breakfast. While he was eating, Margaret came down. "You had a pretty restless night."

"Yes!" But he did not elaborate. He had decided he would call Clewiston and pursue the deal on his own. After finishing breakfast, he went into the study and opening a drawer, took out a piece of paper with Clewiston's phone number. Picking up the phone, he placed a call to Clewiston. When it was answered, he asked for Sir Arthur. When Sir Arthur picked up the call he said, "Sir, my name is David Fulham and as you may remember my telling you, when Sir Charles Grayson was alive, we discussed my buying the American Laminating Co. I understand that he never mentioned it to you and that is unfortunate. However, I still would like to acquire the company and wonder if we can set something in motion toward that end?"

"Mr. Fulham, I do not believe the Board of Directors are so inclined at this time, but to do so I will have to bring this up before them. What I will need from you will be a formal proposal specifying the monetary amount and outlining the details and method of payment. After I receive that information, I will place it before the them for their consideration and approval."

"Fine. Thank you, Sir. I will prepare my proposal and send it to you."

"By the way, Mr. Fulham, what is your interest in American Laminating and why do you wish to acquire it?"

"Formerly, I was president of that firm having built it up from a small operation to the size it is today. Presently I am not pleased with the people who are running the company nor the direction it is taking. It is my opinion that with better leadership and direction, the company has a tremendous potential for growth. I also feel I am more qualified in that direction to achieve that potential given the opportunity."

"Well, Mr. Fulham, thank you for your interest. Send me your proposal and I will pass it on to the board for their consideration."

After hanging up, Sir Arthur thought, *This is some peacock. He certainly is not ashamed to blow his horn. I wonder what those working under him thought of him. I think I should like to talk to Mr. Wells and learn a little more about our* Mr. *Fulham.*

Buzzing his secretary, Miss Mardsden, he instructed her to call Mr. John Wells at American Laminating in the United States for him. When Skip came to the phone, he said, "Good morning, Mr. Wells. I just finished talking to Mr. Fulham and he indicated he wishes to acquire American Laminating. Do you know anything about that?"

"No, but that rather surprises me, Sir, because when he was here some time ago, he suggested that he and I buy the company. Apparently now he has decided too pursue the sale on is own."

"He also inferred that he expanded the company to its present size from a small operation."

"That is partially true, but the business success we are now enjoying is not due to him. On the contrary, he stifled all technological developments while he was here."

"Did Sir Charles indicate to you that the board wished to divest themselves of the company?"

"No, Sir. On the contrary it was because Mr. Fulham allied himself with two former members of the board that Sir Charles felt this a betrayal and fired all three."

"Do you think if he gets the company, the company will expand?"

"No, Sir, I do not...I believe he will stop the production of several products we are now running because they are not highly profitable items. I also believe that should he return, several of our key people will leave."

"Mr. Wells, do you have any interest in purchasing the company?"

"The prospect is intriguing, but in all honesty I have not been in the organization long enough to warrant taking on such a big liability. My staff and I are grateful for our positions here and feel that we owe BEL our loyalty. However, should the board seriously consider selling the company, then to preserve the gains we have made and to protect my employees, I will consider submitting a counter proposal for the board's consideration."

"I thank you, Mr. Wells. I appreciate your honesty and I will get back to you."

After he hung up, Skip thought, *Why that weasel! He's trying to steal the company from under us. Before I let that happen, we'll submit a proposal and beat him at his own game.*

I'll discuss this at the next staff meeting and then get Glen to contact some brokers to see what's required to raise a stock issue.

***

Thumbing through his phone book, Dave found the number for his friend Cal Jones and dialed the number. When Cal answered, he said, "Cal, this is Dave Fulham. What kind of information do I have to give you to arrange for a stock issue?"

"Why? What do you want to buy?"

"I'm thinking of possibly buying the company I previously worked for from its British owners."

"Oh, you no longer work there?"

"No, I left earlier this year."

"What kind of money are we talking about?"

"I really don't know. They do about $20 million a year."

"To be able to set a fair price, we will need the balance sheets for the past ten years. This should show all their assets, liabilities, profit margins, also their status in the markets they serve. We also should have an idea of their goals and their projections for new products and markets."

"You need all that?"

"Yes, to help you set a fair price and prepare the data necessary to interest prospective investors. If, on the other hand, you set a price they agree to, then we still need the data for the prospectus. What will be the terms of your offering?"

"I thought I would borrow a sum against my house for an initial down payment to bind the agreement, then give them whatever money we get for the stock. Finally we pay off any remaining balance over a period of several years from the profits we make."

"No, Dave. It doesn't work that way. The stock issue raises the full amount or you give them what you do raise, then give them shares of stock as equity for the remainder."

"How long does it take to float a stock issue?"

"Depends on the sale of the shares. It could take a couple of weeks or then again several months. It's hard to tell."

"OK. Thanks, Cal. I'll get back to you."

After Dave hung up he thought, Rats! How am I going to get ten years of the company's annual reports? Let me call Glen. Maybe he can help me.

Dialing up Glen, when he answered, he said, "Hi, Glen. This is Dave Fulham. How are you doing? How're the family and the kids?"

"OK, Dave. How about yourself? What are you doing these days?"

"I have my own company brokering used machinery. Things could be better, but with the state of the economy, we're slow. I was wondering if I could ask you for a favor?"

"Sure, Dave. What do you want?"

"Skip and I are thinking about buying American Laminating from BEL and what I need is whatever annual statements you have issued for the past ten years. We need it to give to the broker who is going to arrange a stock issue for us."

"I'll have to ask Mr. Wells and if he agrees, I'll send them to you."

"Well, he is so busy I didn't want to bother him with any details since I'm doing all the legwork."

"I still will have to get his o.k."

"Yes, of course I know you do, but tell you what. Don't bother. I'll get them from him when I see him next week. Thanks anyway." With that he hung up. Now he thought, Another fool! There must be another way that I can get that information.

CHAPTER 15

LIZ WAS IN SKIP'S office discussing her projects. They had bought the printers needed and planned to install them the following week. The incinerator project was moving along nicely. They had narrowed the field down to two bidders and were waiting for the revised bids to come in. The underground solvent storage tanks on the west side of the building had been removed and because they were so deteriorated, new double walled tanks were purchased and were presently being installed at the front of the building. She continued to relate details of the project and the progress they were making when the phone rang.

Picking it up he said, "Skip here."

"Skip, this is Jess. Can I come up? We got trouble."

"What kind of trouble?"

"Chelsea Foods just cancelled all their orders and just refused a whole shipment."

"Jesus! Why? What the hell happened?"

"They say they've had lots of complaints of food poisoning."

"Food Poisoning? Come on up and bring Bob with you."

Hanging up the phone, he said, "Jeez! That's all we need now is an expensive law suit!"

When Jess and Bob arrived Liz wanted to leave, but Skip said, "Stay, Liz. You're part of this group." Turning to Jess he said, "What's this all about?"

"I don't know, Skip. I got a call from shipping telling me that Chelsea Foods refused our last shipment and are sending back the whole trailer load."

"Did he say why?"

"No, he didn't know but I was told they refused our shipment. When I called Mel Slater, my counterpart at Chelsea, he said it was because of food poisoning. Apparently they've had complaints from some of their customers."

"How does that involve us? We're not shipping food to them."

"They don't know what the problem is so they've stopped the whole operation. Until they find out what the problem is, we're on hold."

"What do you think, Bob?"

"I don't know. When we shipped them the samples, they said they looked good and gave us an order."

"So where do we go from here?"

"There's nothing we can do, Skip, until they find out what the problem is. Believe me they are more worried than we are. They are sending samples down to an independent lab for testing and we have to wait for the results. Meanwhile we've stopped running that product until we know one way or the other."

"Jess, can you run something else in the interim?"

"Not really. This product runs on the narrow laminators and we have nothing else we can run at this time. We'll just have to wait for an answer from them."

"Jeez, that's all we need now with Dave still buzzing around in the wings."

"What should I do, Skip, furlough the operators since we don't know how long before we have an answer?"

"No, put them on something else and let's hope we get an answer soon."

After the boys left, he got back with Liz and she finished her report.

"Good job, Liz."

"Thanks, Skip. What do you think is wrong at Chelsea Foods?"

"I don't know. I hope we get an answer soon. I don't want to lose that business and certainly don't want any lawsuits. They can bankrupt a company."

After Liz left he remained at his desk thinking about things in general and what had been achieved since he came. He was pleased with how well the company was doing short of the news he just received. Then he thought about what Dave had asked him regarding buying the company. He wasn't ready for this big step. Elizabeth had been right. Now he thought, *What am I going to tell Dave if he calls?*

***

Several days went by and still no answer was forthcoming from Chelsea Foods. Skip was truly worried. *No one ever knows the outcome of lawsuits and they could be devastating to the company* .Finally in desperation, he called Bob.

"Bob, any word from Chelsea? We can't go on like this. We have to have some answers. Why don't you high tail it down there tomorrow and get with the Chelsea people. See what you can find out. Hopefully, they may have some answers by the time you get there. All we can do here is keep our fingers crossed and hope they found out what's wrong."

***

Rose came in and asked Skip, "What do you want to do for Christmas?"

"To tell you the truth, I hadn't thought about it. What did you do last year?"

"Dave had us clean out an area in the plant. Then a caterer came in, set up tables, and alternately served us a ham or turkey dinner. For a door prize he gave several $100 amounts to the men or women holding the lucky tickets. He made a speech thanking us all for our efforts during the past year and indicated we should strive a little harder to meet our goals in the coming year. The party started at 1:00 PM and at 3:00 PM we returned to work."

"That was it?"

"Yes."

"Well, that wasn't much of a party. Tell you what. Get together with some of the other girls in the office and plan a real one. Rent a hall, order a nice dinner, and invite all the employees including their spouses, their children, or their significant others. Christmas is for the children, so I want a real Santa to hand out presents to all the boys and girls. For the presents use you best judgment and spend $15 or $20 each. I want it to be a Christmas party they'll all enjoy and remember."

***

Dave had been annoyed all week ever since he made the call to Cal. To think some lousy pieces of paper were holding up all his plans. Somebody must have copies of the annual reports, but who? Then a thought struck him. *Sir Charles certainly had received them. Chances are, after he read them, he probably discarded them. Maybe not. Maybe it is worth a shot in the dark.* Once again he dialed Sir Charles's number. When someone answered, he inquired, "Whom am I speaking to?"

"This is Williams."

"Oh, Williams, this is Dave Fulham. Do you remember me?"

"Indeed I do, Sir."

"If you cleaned out Sir Charles's personal papers, do you remember seeing any copies of the annual report of the American Laminating Co.?"

"Oh, I would not know anything about that. Perhaps young Mr. Charles can be of some assistance. He handles the estate now."

"Is he there?"

"One moment, Sir, and I'll get him."

When young Charles came to the phone, he repeated his question.

"Mr. Fulham, when I cleaned out my father's desk, I segregated all those papers that I felt were of some importance and sent them on to Sir Arthur Clewiston. Those that I felt had little or no importance I gave to Williams to discard. Vaguely I recall seeing one or two of the reports you mention. They would be part of the collection I gave to Williams to destroy."

"Do you know if they have already been destroyed?"

"No, I do not but Williams can answer that question. I will call him and you can ask him directly."

When Williams answered, he said, "Williams, Mr. Charles says they might be in that group of papers he gave you to get rid of. Have they been burned or destroyed yet?"

"Yes, Sir. I believe they have. They were bundled into several bags and given to the gardener to burn with the rest of the trash. I am sorry, Sir."

"Thank you, Williams." Hanging up the phone he muttered, "Damn it! Everything happens to me. What am I going to do now? That fool Glen! I'm sure he told Skip I wanted the annual reports. If I were Skip, I wouldn't release those reports to me either." As he sat there drumming his fingers on his pad and staring into space, Margaret came in.

"Trouble, Hon?"

"Some things aren't going right."

"You're still not thinking about buying that company are you?"

"Well, I was but it seems like it is out of the question now."

"Look, Hon, we're pretty well fixed. We own our home, have two kids in good schools, have some money in savings and investments, and you own you own business. Why do we want this big headache?"

"You don't understand, Margaret."

"No, I guess I don't. It's just that I can't see you racking your brain over something that's not going to bring us anymore happiness." With that she left.

Maybe she's right, but damn it, I brought that company from what it was as a baby to what it is now and it grates on me to see all those profits go overseas. I hate to do it. I guess I'll have to talk to Skip again. Maybe together we can work something out.

***

For the past several days Skip had been pouring over the reports Bob had left with him regarding possible new products when Glen called and wanted to come up.

"Sure, come on up." As yet he had not heard from Bob and wondered what they had found out, if anything. In any case he determined he would call Bob after Glen left.

When Glen walked in, he said, “Hi, what’s up?”

“Just got a call from Mr. Fulham and he asked for copies of the company’s annual reports for the past ten years. Said you knew all about it.”

“No, I don’t but you didn’t agree to give them to him, did you?”

“No, of course not, at least not without your permission. Tell me, are you trying to buy the company? Is that why you wanted me to contact brokers regarding a stock issue?”

“Partly. When he was in here, Dave suggested that we buy the company together, meaning he and I. Then I found out from Sir Clewiston that he is trying to buy it surreptitiously on his own which is why he is trying to get the information he needs from you.”

“Do you really want to buy it, Skip? It may be a good idea, but there are some drawbacks.”

“I know. That’s why I had you contact some brokers to find out how it could be done. He can’t be part of the deal because he would either want to be president again or chairman of the Board of Directors that we will have to establish. I can’t allow either so there’s the problem.”

As they continued to talk, the phone rang and Rose said, “Skip, Bob is on the line and he sounds very excited.”

Picking up the phone, he uttered, “Excuse me, Glen. Yes, Bob?”

“Skip, good news! It’s not a poisoning problem, but one of solvent odor retention.”

“What! What does that mean?”

“The odor of the solvents that we are using either for the printing or the laminating is being retained by the substrate and getting into the food they wrap with it.”

“Well, that still sounds like a serious problem.”

“Not so bad, Skip. I think all we have to do is run the web through a dryer that can scrub the web with the impingement of high velocity air. Then I believe we’ll be OK.”

"Gee, Bob. That's great. I hope you're right. When are you coming back?"

"I'll be back tomorrow. I just want to find out a bit more about the testing they did and the results. See you then. Bye."

When Skip hung up, Glen asked, "What was that all about?"

"We got back a whole trailer load of pallets from Chelsea Foods and they cancelled all their orders."

"I heard, but why?"

"Apparently some customers complained of food poisoning."

"Food Poisoning? Wow! That is serious."

"But Bob found out that all it was, was solvent retention odor and he knows how to get rid of it so we should be OK. Getting back to you, I don't know if I want to buy the company because of the amount of money involved, but at the same time, I don't want Dave to purchase it either. That's my dilemma. Did you find out anything from any brokers?"

"Yes, the same thing Dave is asking for is what they require from us. It's a big undertaking, Skip, and I would seriously think about it before going ahead."

"Thanks, Glen. I appreciate your advice. Let me think a little more about it and then we can get together if we are to start the ball rolling."

After Glen left, Skip sat at his desk thinking, *Do I really want to buy the company? What will I gain? More money, some prestige, a number of shares of stock that I will own, but more than that, a big liability. I have no children that I have to take care of and Moira is gone. She got my house and a good deal of my money. No, other than that I will be a bit richer, I really don't see any advantage in assuming a big liability to own a piece of the company. But how can I stop Dave from getting it? He's not the right person to acquire it. What should I do?*

It was a big problem and he knew he would spend more sleepless nights wrestling with the problem.

CHAPTER 16

FRIDAY MORNING WAS COLD and sunny. The throes of winter had arrived. After another restless night, Skip had arrived at the office early. Sitting at his desk he was going through the mail in his in box when Rose arrived.

"Good morning, Skip."

"Good morning, Rose."

"Another restless night?"

"Yeah, too many things on my mind."

"Still thinking about buying the company?"

"That and some other things. I really don't have the money needed to buy this company. If I do, it will mean going deep into debt which I don't want to do. Dave is scooting around in the wings and if he buys it, some nice people are going to lose their jobs. I can't let that happen. Then this business with Chelsea Foods, I don't want to lose their business. I hope Bob is right and has the answer. But most of all, I go home to an empty house and that's not good. When you live alone in a big empty house, you tend to brood."

"Why don't you get back to doing some of the things you did before your wife left you? You could get back to playing golf again. You said you were a pretty good golfer."

"I was… I was even a pretty good skier. As a matter of fact, I even taught skiing."

"You did? So there you are. You could pick up the pieces and go from there."

"You're right, Rose. Maybe with the new year I'll put it all behind me and make a fresh start doing some of the things I did previously. Who knows what may happen."

Just then Bob popped into Rose's office heading for Skip's when Rose spied him and said, "Here's Bob."

"Come on in, Bob. I hope you bring good news."

Entering, the first thing he said was, "Yes, it is. It was merely a solvent odor retention problem and we're going to be alright, Skip. All we have to do is better dry the adhesive we use to laminate our product before we ship it."

"I'm certainly glad to hear that. I had visions of many lawsuits which we certainly don't need especially at this time. Explain to me what it's all about."

"No, Skip, there won't be any lawsuits. Things got blown a bit out of proportion because of the solvent odor. You see, after laminating the paper and foil a certain amount of solvent odor is retained by the coated substrate after it is wound into a roll. The solvent is the liquid component of the adhesive we apply in laminating the paper to the foil. In printing, the solvent is also the liquid vehicle in the ink used to print onto the web.

"Some foods, namely those that contain fats or oils like butter, chocolate, cheese, and meats tend to retain the odor from the materials they are wrapped in. In this case it was the odor of the MEK (methyl ethyl ketone) we used as the solvent vehicle in the adhesive we make to laminate the paper to the foil.

"After Chelsea Foods received many complaints, they decided to test the food wrapping material. What they did was cut samples of our substrate into pieces and place them into the chamber of a gas chromatograph for testing. What they found out was that the odor retention from our products was in the magnitude of 50ppm (parts per million) which is high. Some people have noses that are very sensitive and can detect odors down to 12ppm. In our case it was the odor retention of 50ppm that caused the problem. To eliminate the objectionable odor transmitted to the foods wrapped in our substrates, all we have to do is reduce the retained odor down to less than 5ppm. This we can do through better drying. Samples we sent out to be scrubbed came back with readings of 0 to 1ppm. Not only that, but the chromatograph was able to distinguish the difference in the specific gravities of the solvents between the alcohol used in the printing ink and the MEK used in our adhesive."

"Very interesting! Is it possible to achieve the results they need?"

"Yes, but not with the equipment we have now. What we have to do is install an after-dryer in the laminating line that can scrub the web, so to speak. The after-dryer uses a high velocity stream of heated air that is impinged on the web which in effect dries the web much better thus reducing any residual solvent odor."

"That's all. Then what was all that about food poisoning?"

"There was no poisoning. Some people got sick because of the chemical odor in the food and thought they were being poisoned."

"What can we do with all the product that was returned? Must we scrap it?"

"No, I have made arrangements to send it out to a printing company. These people have the equipment we require to do the job we need. I am sure we can get down to 2ppm or below with no problem and reship the product we've produced."

"That's great, Bob. Give Jim and his engineering department the specs they will need so that they can come up with the dryer we will require."

"I already have. They figure the dryer we need must be at least fifteen feet long and have the capability of delivering an impingent velocity of 15,000 fpm (feet per min.) at an air temperature of 280 degrees F (Fahrenheit)."

"Fantastic, Bob! You did a great job. You sure have taken a big load off my mind. Thanks ever so much."

After he left, Skip thought, *Well, that's one less headache to worry about.*

***

Christmas Eve had arrived and everyone was excited about the party. The girls had done a beautiful job of hanging decorations throughout the office and plant. A magnificent tree, decked out with all kinds of ornaments, stood in the main entrance lobby. Skip had closed the plant early for the holiday and there was no doubt that the Christmas spirit prevailed all through the plant.

Work had stopped at 1:00 PM to give everyone a chance to go home and change for the party which was scheduled to start at 4:00 PM. The results were better than an Easter parade. The women were ravishing in their finery and the children looked absolutely splendid in their outfits.

Skip was totally pleased with what he saw. Even the banquet hall was nicely decorated. The girls had done a beautiful job. The dinner was superb, turkey with all the trimmings. The open bar served beer, wine or cocktails to the adults and sodas to the children and gaiety pervaded the entire hall.

Before the dinner was over, Skip rapped for attention. Then getting up he started speaking. "Christmas is a joyful time and as I gaze around this room I see a sea of happy faces. I came as a stranger into you midst, not knowing anything about this company, its people, or what you do and how you do it. After these several months of my being here, I now feel I am part of this family. This year has been a good one for us, despite the economic conditions of the country, through your efforts. I hope that we will continue to prosper. We have embarked on some new products in areas that tend to be more stable. Hopefully, we can continue and expand on that path. Our goal is to reach $35 million in sales. I think we can achieve and perhaps surpass that goal. Toward that end, I authorized Mr. Overman to include an extra $100 in each of your paychecks. It isn't much, but it's this company's way and mine of saying thank you for your efforts. I especially want to thank Rose and all the rest of the people who helped make this a wonderful party. To all of you, I wish a very Merry Christmas and the very best in the New Year.

"Now if the children will line up, I believe Santa has a little something for all of them. But before they do, will the holders of the following numbers … 4, 23, 54, and 112 come forward. I think Santa has something extra…$250. for each of you. You lucky people!"

The silence in the banquet hall was shattered by the thunderous applause of the group for their new leader. They were proud of him, but no, it was more than that. It was their way of showing their affection and admiration to their boss, a very caring person.

CHAPTER 17

JANUARY HAD COME AND gone and this was the middle of February. American Laminating was humming along. Even Dave had done quite well. He had sold several pieces of equipment to Apex Printing and was quite pleased with his company's performance, but the purchase of American Laminating was still gnawing at him despite his conversation with Margaret. He still felt this was the thing to do. But how? Without the annual reports which detailed American's performance over the years, it would be neigh on impossible to raise the money needed to swing any kind of deal. But how to get them? He knew Skip would not release any information to him. What could he do?

He had estimated that it would take between $15 million and $18 million to buy the company. At least that's what he was prepared to offer. Without the reports, however, he would not be able to get anyone interested in his quest to raise that sum.

No, he wouldn't be able to float any kind of a stock issue on something he didn't own. Like it or not, he guessed he'd have to go see Skip.

Then he thought, *I have a better idea. I'll visit the office when no one's around and sneak into Glen's office to get what I need. If I go there after 5:30 PM, the office will be empty so it shouldn't be too difficult to get into his office, I think. If it doesn't work out, I'll play it be ear. Now let's see when's good day...Friday because everybody leaves early to get a head start for the weekend.*

***

It was 5:40 when Dave pulled into the parking lot at the entrance to the reception lobby. Carefully looking around to make sure no one saw him, he left his car and entered the lobby. Walking rapidly he went through the door to the staircase which lead to the second floor. Carefully opening the door of the second floor, he looked down the hall and saw no one. Entering the hall he walked rapidly down the hall to Glen's office. Knocking on the door and receiving no answer, he entered. Closing the door, he moved rapidly to the file cabinets against the wall where he saw none were locked. Opening the drawer marked "A", he rummaged through the files until he found a folder labeled "annual reports." Leafing through the folder he managed to find reports only for the last five years. Taking one copy of each of the years, he rummaged further in the drawer for earlier copies, but there were none. Either they were discarded or placed in archives elsewhere. Well, he thought these would have to do. Putting everything back to order, he closed the drawer. Folding the reports, he put them into his breast pocket. His heart was beating like a trip hammer. Saying to himself, *So far so good. Let's see if I can just get out of here without being seen.* Cautiously he opened the door and looked down the hallway. Again there was no one. He was in luck. Exiting the office, he closed the door and walked back to the door of the staircase which lead down to the lobby and went down. As luck would have it, as he exited into the lobby, who should he encounter but Hank Norris, the watchman, coming to lock up.

"Oh Hello, Mr. Fulham. What are you doing here?"

"Came to see Mr. Wells, but he isn't in."

"No, they all leave early on Friday. Is there something you want or want me to tell him?"

"No thanks, Hank. I'll call him Monday."

"Sure thing, Mr. Fulham."

"By the way, how's the family, Hank?"

"They're all OK, Mr. Fulham. My oldest boy Steve is just starting college."

"That's great. Where's he going?"

"Stevens Tech. He wants to study engineering."

"That's great! He couldn't have picked a better school or profession."

"Glad to hear you say that, Mr. Fulham, because I knew you was an engineer."

"Well, goodnight, Hank. My best to you and the family. I'll call Skip Monday."

"Goodnight, Mr. Fulham. I'll finish locking up after you leave."

Walking back to his car, Dave thought, *Boy, that was close, but I think I handled it well. Maybe I should call Skip Monday. This way I'm covered if Hank happens to mention I was around.*

As he drove away, he started to think. *Now that I have these five reports, I'll have to call Cal and see what he thinks. Maybe we have enough information to proceed.* Glancing at his watch, he saw it was already after 6:00. *It's too late to call him now. I'll have to call him Monday morning.*

***

On Monday at 11:00 AM Dave went into the study and put in a call to Cal Jones, his brokerage friend. After a long wait, Cal finally answered. "You're a hard guy to get a hold of. Are you that busy?"

"Yes, this whole morning has been hectic. Literally the phones have been ringing off the hook."

"That bad, heh?"

"Worse. The market's been extremely volatile all morning. People don't know what to do about their investments. The economic conditions are driving them crazy. I've reached a point where even I don't know how to advise them."

"Maybe this wasn't a good time to call you."

"No, it's OK. What's on your mind, Dave?"

"Remember when I spoke to you about buying up American Laminating, Co.? You told me I had to give you the annual reports for the last ten years."

"Yes, I remember. So?"

"Well, I was only able to get the reports for the last five."

"That may be OK. We can probably work around with what we have. As president you can give us whatever else we will need."

"No, I'm no longer president or work for the company."

"What? You're no longer with the company and you want to buy it? How do you propose to do that?"

"I thought you could work that out."

"Look, Dave, I'm a stock broker, not a magician. When you run a company, you can put it and its assets up as collateral against a stock issue. But if you're not part of the company in a very responsible position, how can you buy it? What kind of money are we talking about anyway and how much do you have?"

"Fifteen to eighteen million dollars and I can probably come up with about a half million on my home and personal assets and maybe another half million against my company, Atlas Machinery. The rest I figured we would get as a loan from some large bank or lending company. We would then use the money we get from the loan to buy the company from the owners. The loan would then be paid off using the cash we have and the money we raise from the sale of the stock."

"That's a lot of scratch to come up with for a relatively unknown company."

"They're a good company, Cal, with a lot of potential."

"Maybe so, but to try and sell it, that's another story."

"Have you any better suggestions?"

"Yes, forget it."

"Why?"

"The way the market is right now and with the tight money situation we're going through, there is no way we can raise that kind of capital. The big boys are all in trouble and waiting for governmental handouts to keep them alive. None are in any position to make big loans at this time."

"As bad as that?"

"Worse."

"Gee, I hate to lose this opportunity if it is possible."

"Dave, save yourself a big headache. Maybe at a much later date when things have settled down, you may have a chance, but now, no way."

Thoroughly disappointed with the news, he said, "OK, Cal. Thanks for the info." Hanging up the phone he remained seated for a few moments thoroughly depressed. The plan he had worked out seemed so simple and easy, but now he was thwarted by the country's economics. Then he thought, *Maybe I should call another broker. No, the chances are the answer would be the same.*

As he left the study and entered the living room, he was spied by Margaret. Seeing the expression on his face she asked, "Bad news?"

"Sort of."

"Dave, you're not still agonizing over buying your old company, are you?"

"Well, I was just talking to a broker about it and he said to forget it because this is a bad time to consider it."

"Oh, Honey, I don't know why you want to beat your head against the wall. We have a roof over our head that's paid for, two cars in the garage that we don't owe any money on, all our bills are paid up to date. Why do we need this big headache. I'm sure it's going to take a lot of money."

"Yes, it will."

"Who needs it? We won't live or sleep any better. As a matter of fact, we may sleep a lot worse with that big debt hanging over our head. Do you realize that instead of just you and your secretary, you now will have a new bunch of people to worry about? How will you feel if you have to shut down operations and lay people off or have bills to pay when money is slow or doesn't come in at all?"

"I know, but it's like a child I raised. I took it from a small two-bit operation to the big company it is today."

"And you did a good job while it lasted, but it's gone. It doesn't belong to you anymore. Concentrate on the company you now have and be a lot happier. Do something you always wanted to do and enjoy yourself."

Then he thought, *She is right. Why do I need to take on a big company? Is it all just to satisfy my ego, gain a little more prestige? No, I'm happy as I am. We've had a good life together and we have enough money to pass onto the kids. I never realized how wise she is. You live with a person and you take a lot of things for granted without giving any of it a second thought. This wonderful woman deserves a lot more. I'm going to revive that spark of love we both had and we'll do more things together. Travel, maybe even play golf together.* Walking over to her, he took her in his arms and kissed her.

"What was that for?"

"For being the true brains of this outfit. You're absolutely right and I love you for it."

"Well, that's a word I haven't heard very often."

"I know. I should tell it to you more often for I do love you even though perhaps I haven't shown it." Seeing a tear form in her eye he asked, "Why are you crying? Have I said something I shouldn't have?"

"No, you big ape. Go do what you have to do. You wouldn't understand."

But she was right. He didn't understand, but now he knew he was going to call Skip and tell him he wasn't interested in buying the company anymore and if he, Skip, was still interested, he would have to go it alone. *Better yet I'll go tell him personally.*

CHAPTER 18

SKIP WAS IN HIS office discussing the details of the start-up of the new incinerator with Jim Porter, Elizabeth, and Ken Fowler. All the necessary testing had been completed and the system was ready to go. Looking around at the three Skip said, "I called all of you here for a job well done. The whole system looks magnificent and I appreciate the effort you all put into it which I'm sure was considerable. At least now we can rest easier in the thought that we no longer are poisoning ourselves and our neighbors. I feel better that we at least have done our part to reduce emissions and comply with the environmental clean air standards."

"When do you want to start up, Skip?" asked Jim.

"I was thinking…," when he was interrupted by Rose. "Yes, Rose?"

"Mr. Fulham is downstairs and would like to see you."

"Tell him to come on up." Then turning to the group he said, "We can finish this later. Then I'll tell you what I have in mind."

Elizabeth, looking at Skip said, "I wonder what he wants."

"Probably wants my answer to his suggestion of buying the company."

"Oh!" piped up Jim. "I didn't know you were considering buying the company."

"I wasn't until he brought it up."

When Dave entered and seeing the three there, he extended his hand and cordially greeted Liz with, "Hello, Liz. How's the family?"

"They're all well, thank you, Dave."

Then turning to Jim he said, "How are the triplets? They must be what... three years now?"

"Almost three. Their birthday comes up soon."

"That's great! I'll bet you and Mary have your hands full."

"You can say that again, but you know it really is something to watch them grow."

Then facing Ken, "How's the leg? I was sorry to hear you banged it up pretty badly in an accident with your bike."

"Yeah, broke it in several places, but it's coming along. I still have a little trouble on cold or damp days."

Then turning to Skip, "I hope I haven't interrupted anything?"

"We were just discussing the startup of our new incinerator."

"As I drove up, I saw it. It looks pretty impressive. I'll bet that cost a pretty penny!"

"About two and a half million all told."

"Whew! That much? Well, I guess it was only a question of time. We were running out of emissions credits when I was around."

Taking their leave and saying goodbye to Dave, the trio left.

"Have a seat, Dave. What brings you here?"

"I came to see you Friday, but you were gone."

"Yeah, Hank left a note for me. Sorry I missed you. I had an early date with some guys I play golf with."

"Are you any good?"

"Shoot in the low 80's most of the time."

"That's not bad. I try to get out on the course whenever I can, but some of the guys I used to play with are gone now so it's hit and miss with me. Maybe you and I can play a round sometime. How are you guys doing?"

"Not bad. Some of the products Bob came up with have really taken off. How about you?"

"I've had a pretty good year. I just sold some pieces of equipment to Apex Printing. Apparently like your business, theirs is taking off too. But I'm glad you guys are doing great."

"Yes, it looks like we're going to make our goal of $35 million this year."

"I can't tell you how happy I am to hear you say that. You know this company was like a baby that I raised. You've done a good job, Skip, and I can see why your people admire you. I don't know. Maybe I was too blind or stubborn to see the relative merits of some of the stuff Bob developed. Apparently they've turned out to be winners. But, that aside, I'll tell you why I came. Have you given any more thought to my suggestion of buying the company?"

"Well, I thought about it and it probably is a good idea. But to tell the truth, I don't have the money it would take to see it through. I went through a painful divorce and my wife got the house, a car and most of the cash I had, so to take on a big debt like this leaves me cold."

"I hear you, Skip, and I'm sorry to hear you're in financial straits, but you know the trick was to buy using other people's money."

"I wish I knew how!"

"Well, it can be done, but perhaps this may not be the best time to try. What I came to tell you is that I no longer am interested in buying the company. I think I have enough on my plate with my own small company rather than go looking for some more. I've decided not to try."

"To tell you the truth, Dave, I really was not interested in buying until you suggested it. I was also wrestling with a dilemma. If we bought it together, what would your position be? I wouldn't want to give up the presidency. Then what would your position be? Not knowing much about you, I wouldn't be comfortable with you over me as chairman of the board."

"I can understand that. In your position I would probably feel exactly the same way. I had a long talk with Margaret and that wise woman made me see that what we don't need is a big burden on our heads."

"You know, Dave, when I mentioned it to Liz, she said the same thing. I guess women think a lot more differently than we do. It probably stems from the fact that they see security as a more important issue. Maybe that's the right way because while we try to protect them, in the long run they really protect us.

"The reason I had Jim, Liz, and Jess up here was to mark the startup our new incinerator with a celebration. I would like to invite some of our neighbors and perhaps some local politicos in. I would also like you here to share in this moment of joy because in a way, as the former president, you were part of it."

"I'd like that and I will be here."

"As soon as we get all the details ironed out, I'll send you an invitation."

"You know since you are a golfer, maybe we can get together for a few rounds?"

"I'm sure we will. Thanks for coming by and I'll look forward to seeing you."

As Dave left, each was equally happy with the thought that he had found a new friend. Surprised at Dave's visit, and even more surprised at his answer, Skip remained seated at his desk for some time staring out the window before he recalled Elizabeth, Jim, and Ken to thrash out details of the program he planned for the incinerator introduction. It would be a gala event, one which the neighborhood would long remember.

CHAPTER 19

JOHN, ON HIS WEEKLY tour around the plant, stopped by laminator #3. Operators there were busy cleaning up the laminator and preparing it for its next run. Carts with rolls of material were strung out in the room out of the way and outside waiting to be rolled in as needed. Jose was positioned at the laminator cleaning the coating rolls with rags soaked in solvent. The roll was turning as he was wiping it and he was breathing in the fumes of MEK. When Skip saw this, he yelled to him. "José, get out of that machine. Why don't you have a mask on?"

"Well, it was only going to be for a few minutes and I thought…"

"I don't care what you thought. I don't want anyone doing any roll cleaning without facemasks. Don't you realize that you are breathing in deadly fumes and while you may not feel anything now, in several years you will be experiencing not only lung problems but mental problems as well? Please, for your sake, always wear the mask. And another thing, please turn the rolls by hand. You know it doesn't take much while the machine is running for you to get your hand caught into the machine. You could lose your hand or even worse, your arm before anyone can stop the machine. I'd hate to see that happen. So be more careful."

"You're right, Skip. I didn't think. It won't happen again."

"I hope not, not only for your sake, but mine."

After staying a little longer watching the operators prepping the machine, he left to continue his walk through the rest of the plant. As he walked he thought, *I have seen several people with injuries that resulted from carelessness or little thought. I don't want any to happen here. I'll have to tell Jess and Ken to have the supervisors be more alert and vigilant.* As he continued on, he was pleased with what he saw. The plant was humming and spic and span, everything seemed to be where it belonged, commendations definitely were in order to all personnel. He was surprised, as he continued his tour, how friendly everyone was. This was more than respect for him because he was the boss. No, this was genuine friendliness and he could detect it in all the people he spoke with. These were his people; they had accepted him and now they were his family.

***

As he passed Rose's office on his way back to his own office, Rose called, "Oh, Skip!"

"Yes, Rose."

"There's a lady here to see you."

"Who is she?"

"I don't know. She wouldn't say."

"What does she want?"

"She wouldn't say only that she has to see you. It's important."

"That's strange. She wants to see me, says it's important, but won't give her name or say what she wants?"

"What should I do?"

"Well, the only way to find out who she is and what she wants is to send her up." He returned to his office and was seated at his desk when Moira appeared.

Entering his office she said, "Hello, John!"

"Moira! This is a surprise. What brings you here?"

"John, I must talk to you."

"This sounds ominous." Pointing to the settee he said, "Please sit down. Now tell me what this is all about. Why have you come here?"

"John, I have been such a fool."

"Now Moira, we all make mistakes or say some things we regret, but that's life. That's no reason to berate yourself or feel recrimination. Tell me what's troubling you. Why do you feel so foolish?"

"Can we go someplace private to talk?"

"We can talk here privately; just close that door." Then pushing a button on his intercom, he said, "Rose, hold all my calls and I'm not to be disturbed by anyone. There now, we're completely private. Now what's this all about? Why are you so depressed?"

"I have been such a fool. I did not realize that as happy as I was in my own little world, that we had serious problems in our marriage or that you were unhappy in your job and wanted to leave it. I should have paid more attention to you and been more sympathetic."

"Well, that's water over the dam. Now you have your freedom and can do all the things you wish. Many women would be happy to change places with you."

"That's just it. It hasn't brought me any happiness. I'm tired of living alone, eating alone, and sleeping alone. And many nights I cry myself to sleep. I'm afraid to live in the big house all alone at night. Every little noise frightens me."

"But why? You didn't have these problems when I was there. At least you never mentioned anything. Why now?"

"That's just it, John. You were there."

"Yes, I see that now. What happened to all those trips and places you wanted to see?"

"I went and thought I would be happy. I did go to some nice places, places I always dreamed of and met some nice people and saw things I always wanted to see, but you know what? At the end of each day I returned to a lonely hotel room. Oh sure, while on the trips I shared the excitement with the other members on the tour, but it's not the same as when you share it with your own companion. I've had lots of time to think and I don't like living alone any longer. I miss you. I still love you and realize I always have. You're such a good and kind person and always thoughtful of others that I wonder how could I have been so blind. Can you find it in your heart to forgive me and the hurt I've cost you?"

Leaving his desk and moving over to the settee to sit beside her, he said, "Yes, I too know the loneliness of returning to an empty house each night with nothing to look forward to or someone to talk to. It's very depressing and life becomes just a mechanical process. Dear Heart, there is nothing to forgive for I still love you and probably always will. I still cherish those happy moments we spent together, but you seemed to be so unhappy that I reluctantly agreed to the divorce. Now I'm not so sure it was the right and wisest thing to do. I'm sorry to see you are so unhappy. I guess I was so wrapped up in my work that I never gave it a thought that you might not be happy." Then taking her into his arms, he kissed her tenderly. "You know I've missed you and to make up for some of the emptiness in my life, I've embraced the employees of this company. They are my people and have become my family, but I've missed you and thought about you often. I wondered how you were many times and wanted to call, but pride prevented me. In that I guess I was foolish." Once again they kissed and stroked each other's faces and hands in loving tenderness. Looking into her eyes, he said, "How would you like to have dinner with me tonight? We can go to that little Italian restaurant you always liked and maybe pick up the pieces. It certainly is worth a try."

"Yes John, I'd love to. When I think how much I've missed."

"Good! Then it's settled. Let's see if we can get back to where we were. Let me tell Rose we're leaving."

Then grasping her hand he pulled her toward him and putting his arms around her he kissed her again. Rising from the settee, he opened the door to Rose's office and as the two of them stood there holding hands like two school children he said, "Rose, this is Mrs. Wells and we're both leaving perhaps to begin life anew." With that they departed.

***

Luigi's was a small neighborhood restaurant located on a quiet street in the older Italian sector of the town. It wasn't a very large place with fancy décor, but it had a certain quaintness about it. It had two large windows in the front and about twenty tables spaced nicely about the room. Off to the back there was a small bar above which were strung many empty Chianti bottles. The half wall behind the bar gave patrons a view into the open kitchen.

Luigi and Rosa had emigrated to the United States as teenagers. They had first met at their port of embarkation and on the trip over developed a romance between them. Since Luigi had no trade, he got himself a job as a laborer on several construction jobs and through diligence and hard work, had risen to foreman.

Rosa was more fortunate. Her grandmother had taught her to cook and sew as a little girl and in a few years she had become quite a proficient cook and seamstress. Her grandmother, seeing the economic conditions that existed at that time in Italy and the social upheaval that was taking place, decided that there was not much future for a bright girl, one of several of a large family, to remain there. Scraping together the little money she had saved over the years, she gave it to Rosa to pay her way to the land of opportunity. There she could now make something of herself. *Vi mia piccolina e scrivemi qualche notizie ogni tanto. Dio ti benedici e quarda ti.* (Go my little one, write to me occasionally. God bless you and watch over you.) With a heavy heart Rosa left and headed for the new world. A chance meeting on the ship brought Luigi and her together. Then like two brave souls they decided to face the challenges of the new world together. After a year in New York, they decided to marry and in short order had two children, a little boy Michael and a girl Julia.

When Mr. Tomasino died, they decided to take the little cash they had saved and buy his ristorante from his widow. Thus Luigi's was born and it wasn't too much longer before Rosa's reputation spread as a fine cook and the restaurant flourished.

It was a big surprise when Skip and Moira showed up at Luigi's After they entered, Luigi, who was polishing glasses at the bar, spied them and came over. "Ha, Mister Wells. Where you bin? A long time you no come here. You bin away? You and Missa Wells O.K.?"

"Yes, Luigi. It has been a long time. How are Rosa and Michael and Julia?"

"They O.K. Michael is a big lawyer now and Julia she getta married and have two children. Come, please sit down over here." With that he ushered them to a nice table by the window.

"What's good to eat, Luigi?"

"Rosa she make lasagna infornato (baked lasagna) this morning. Very good." And with that he twirled the fingers of his right hand above his lip to a nonexistent mustache. Then he said, "I bring you a nice glass of wine." With that he motioned for the waiter Gino to come over. *"Primo fa un' insalata misto per loro e poi va prende due piatte di lasagna da Rosa e servila."* (First mix a salad for them and then get two plates of lasagna from Rosa and serve it to them.)

As they sat there and ate, like two lovebirds they reminisced over the past. Skip took Moira's hand and said, "Sweetheart, I missed you terribly. I love you and I can't envision life without you. Let's put the past behind us and get remarried right away and start all over." The tears in her eyes were all the answer he needed.

Two weeks later, in a quiet civil ceremony, they were remarried and Skip moved back home to start life anew.

CHAPTER 20

THE BIG DAY FINALLY arrived. The plant looked resplendent with its decorations. The maintenance department had done itself proud. Flags and bunting adorned the chain link fence and colorful streamers ran from the top of the building to the fence. The street between the two buildings had been blocked off and a small raised platform was erected for the speakers to use.

Some large placards had been placed in the windows of several local merchants informing the neighborhood of the event. In addition, invitations had gone out to Harold Nesbitt, director of the state Environmental Protection Agency, Division of Clean Air Standards and to Robert Johnstone, commissioner of Plant Occupational Hazard and Safety, and also to Tom Riley, the director of the local agency for building permits and licenses.

Inside the plant the shipping area had been cleaned out and tables set up so that those attending could sit and enjoy refreshments. There was coffee, tea, and Danish for the adults and ice cream, soda, pretzels, and potato chips for the children.

Outside, tours were arranged for those individuals interested in viewing the installation and hearing either engineering or maintenance personnel describe the function and operation of salient points of the process. The system included the collecting ductwork from the laminators to the baghouse where dust and all foreign matter from the laminators was filtered out of the solvent fumes before they entered the incinerator. Here the fumes were incinerated at 2,000 degrees F and then discharged to the atmosphere. Now the plant was in compliance with Clean Air Standards and thus eliminated the obnoxious odor that previously had pervaded the plant and the surrounding neighborhood for years.

Jim Porter, acting as master of ceremony, greeted the important guests as they arrived and handed them over to designated personnel to show them around the plant. Now they got a chance to see the different machines and what they did or produced and then finally moving outside saw the new incinerator which after all was the object of the party.

When Dave arrived with Margaret, seeing Skip with a group talking to Jim, he walked over to meet them and introduced Margaret. Skip, spying him as he approached said, "Hello, Dave. Glad you could make it. This is Moira, my wife."

"Thank you, Skip," and turning to Margaret he said, "Honey, this is Skip Wells, the new president of the company and his wife." Introductions were made all around and then Dave turning to Skip said, "You've got quite a turnout here."

"Yes, well we tried to reach all we felt might be interested, especially the neighbors who were curious about what we did and who will now benefit from the new equipment."

Everything went well and the party hummed along when finally at 4:00 Jim called for attention. Everyone moved outside to hear the speakers. As in most festivals, the speakers, each in his turn, lauded management for their effort to provide a cleaner and safer environment for the employees and the neighborhood. Some stressed how this set a good example for other industries to follow.

In his turn, Dave related some of the history of the company citing how it had grown from the small mom-and- pop startup by Mr. and Mrs. Jacobs to the big corporation it was now. He ended saying that though he was no longer part of the company, he was glad he had had a hand in guiding it from its infancy through its growth. He was proud to see what the company had achieved under Mr. Wells.

When Skip finally rose, he praised Dave for bringing the company from that small start to the large corporation it was now. Then he described some of the new products they were producing and had under development. The company would grow much larger as it reached out to newer and wider markets. He thanked all the employees for their efforts and devotion, for without it the company would not have achieved the goals it set nor the success they enjoyed. Finally, he concluded with thanking Elizabeth and her committee and all those that participated for doing such a fine job planning and handling the festivities.

When the party finally broke up, all left with a glowing feeling for the company and Skip Wells.

CHAPTER 21

"HELLO, LIZ. THIS IS Jess. Did you get a chance to talk to Jim?"

"No. After I left you I went to see him, but he was having a meeting with his engineers and Ken. I told him what I wanted and he suggested I put it off for this morning. I went up a little while ago and the place was a circus. Mary had come with the triplets and the office was filled with some of the office and sales gals who wanted to hold the kids. Those three little ones are all heart stealers. They were all so cutely dressed and not the least bit shy. I hated to leave. He indicated Mary was going to leave shortly and he would come and join us as soon as she left."

Liz arranged that she, Jess, Ken, and Glen would go up to Skip's office now and Jim could join the group as soon as Mary left. Calling Skip she then told him they were coming up told him what it was all about. On her way to Skip's office, she met

Glen whose office was nearby. As the two entered she said, "Skip, would you prefer we meet here or go into the conference room?"

"No. Let's stay here. We'll wait for the others."

"Jess and Ken are on the way up. Jim will be a little delayed because Mary is here with the triplets."

"Oh, I didn't know they were here."

"Apparently Mary had to bring something in for Jim so she brought the children along."

After they were all seated and waiting for Jim, Skip asked, "What's this about a new machine?"

"The time has come to either purchase some new equipment or up-grade what we have," responded Jess. "Laminator #1 is thirty-one years old and has been running three shifts continuously seven day a week since it was first installed. Indeed a remarkable performance, but now I think we have to either up-grade it or buy something new."

"It's more than that, Skip. It's using a lot of my maintenance budget to keep it running," said Ken. "We have to do a lot of jury rigging to keep it running and we never get the downtime we need to make complete repairs. Besides, drive and control systems have improved dramatically since we got our machines and it is almost sinful to operate ours as we do."

Just then Jim arrived. "Sorry I'm late. Had the family here."

"Yes, I heard. Apparently they create quite a stir when they come," replied Skip.

"Yeah, I know it seems like the whole office staff comes in when they're here. God bless my kids! None of them is shy. You know they are almost three. Mary has taught them a few songs to sing and dance to and when they perform them, they steal your heart. But Tom! That's my boy. He is the apple of my eye."

"I'm happy for you, Jim. Sorry I missed seeing them. Enjoy these moments as much as you can for they disappear all too quickly as the children grow. There will be other moments later on, but these are the precious ones you won't forget. Getting back to what we were discussing, what would a new machine cost?"

"It was indicated that a new laminating line complete with a dryer, winders, a d.c. drive, digital controls, and a printing station would probably run about two million dollars installed."

"Whew! That much?" cried Skip.

"I would guess at least that," replied Jess.

Then the idea of up-grading laminator #1 was discussed. This would include a new higher horsepower dc drive, a new computer control station that would have locked in its memory all the settings to activate and regulate all the controls necessary to run and produce quality products. It would also include speed, tension, temperature, and roll pressure data and the like. They also thought many of the roll bearings should be replaced and all the rolls completely realigned. These were the minimum changes that would be required. Perhaps other changes might be needed as the work proceeded. In addition, a new printer should also be included for those products that would require in-line printing.

"That sounds like a substantial amount of changes. Any idea what it would cost?" asked Skip.

"Conservatively…about a million dollars…but even with good preplanning, the drawback is the considerable downtime required to make the changes."

"That doesn't paint a pretty picture and leaves us with little choice," responded Skip.

Just then the phone rang. Skip picking it up said, "Rose, please hold all my calls. We're in an important meeting."

"This is an urgent call for Jim."

Handing the phone over to Jim, Jim answered, "Jim Porter here. What! …When?…How?…Oh my God!…No, I'll be right there." Handing the phone back to Skip, tears welling in his eyes, he said, "I have to go. Mary and the kids have been in an accident and they've taken her to the hospital."

No shock could have been more profound. The group was electrified, but in short order they gathered around Jim to give him whatever consolation they could. As he prepared to leave, his body shaking uncontrollably and tears streaming down his face, Skip left his chair and grabbing Jim put his arm around his shoulder and said, "You're in no condition to drive. Come on. I'll take you there." Turning to the group he said, "We'll pick this up at another time."

After they left, speculation ran high as to what happened. Liz opened the door to Rose's office and asked, "Rose, do you know who that phone call was from?"

"No, all he said was, 'This is officer Tom Byrnes of the 31st precinct. Is a Mr. James Porter there?'" she answered.

"That's all?"

"Yes, why? What happened?"

Then she related what transpired. Finally looking at the others, she said, "I guess we'll hear what happened when Skip returns."

***

Mercy Hospital was a big sprawling complex that stretched over many acres. It included several large buildings. Among other things, it was a teaching hospital and boasted its facilities, housed the latest most advanced medical equipment, and its medical staff was second to none. This emergency wing was brand-new and always a very busy place.

Arriving at the hospital, Jim and Skip immediately went to the emergency wing and at the reception desk inquired about Mary and the children. The receptionist told them as yet her records were incomplete. But she did know two women and some children were brought in. One woman had died on the way to the hospital and the other was rushed into the operating room. No, she didn't know which was which. She did know that since the children were only shaken and required no treatment, they were released. As to who was in the operating room, they would have to wait until a doctor came out. When Jim asked about where the children were, she didn't know except that they had been released. She then suggested that they speak with the paramedics who were in the coffee shop and they could probably give more information about the accident and perhaps about the children.

As they started to head for the coffee shop, a doctor in operating room dress stopped at the reception desk. When the receptionist pointed to Jim, he came over and said, "Mr. Porter, I'm Doctor Brenner. Your wife is just coming out of surgery now. She was banged up pretty badly in the accident. She sustained several fractures and multiple internal injuries. We did the best we could."

"Can we see her?" asked Jim.

"No. She's in the recovery room now and is still unconscious. Shortly they'll be bringing her up to the intensive care unit. You can see her then."

"She is alright, isn't she?"

"Her condition is very critical and I wouldn't venture a guess. She was hurt pretty badly and has too many complications."

"Oh my God!" moaned Jim.

"Are you a religious man, Mr. Porter? If you are, I would suggest you pray."

"That bad?" said Skip.

"Worse," replied the doctor.

"Jim, since we can't see her yet, let's go find the paramedics. Maybe they can tell what happened to your children."

***

The coffee shop was filled with hospital personnel and friends or relatives of patients. Looking around, Skip saw three paramedics in a booth across the room. Nudging Jim they walked over and asked, "Are you the guys that brought the lady who is in the operating room?"

"No. We brought in a man who had a stroke."

Walking over to a second group, they repeated the question.

When the medic replied, "yes," they asked, "What happened to the three small children who were in the car?"

"I believe they were taken by a policewoman back to the thirty-first precinct," answered one.

"Were they OK?"

"I checked them over pretty thoroughly and apart from their being shaken up a bit and crying, they seemed OK." Then facing Jim, he asked, "Was that lady your wife?"

"Yes," replied Jim.

"She was hurt pretty bad, I hate to say. I don't know if she's going to make it."

With that Jim burst uncontrollably into tears and Skip, as staunch as he was, had wet eyes, too. Seeing the condition of Jim, one of the paramedics suggested that Skip ask one of the doctors to give Jim something to calm him down.

Skip replied, "He'll be OK. It's just that this is such a big shock."

"Yeah. I can imagine. It's a tough break."

Turning to Jim, Skip suggested that while they were waiting to see Mary, he, Skip, would go call Moira and let her know what happened and that he was bringing Jim and all the children home.

"No, Skip," Jim replied. "You've done enough already. I'll pick up the kids and go home."

"You're in no condition to drive or stay home tonight let alone take care of three small children. You and the kids will stay over in our place and tomorrow you can go home, if you like. Wait here while I go call Moira."

Finding a pay phone, Skip called Moira. "Honey, I'm at Mercy Hospital with Jim Porter. His wife Mary was in a bad accident."

"Oh! I'm sorry to hear that. Is she going to be alright?"

"No. She's on the critical list and may not make it."

"Oh my God! That poor man."

"Moira, he is in no condition to go home so I'm bringing them all to stay at our place tonight." Then he suggested that the three small children could sleep in the bed in the guest room and Jim could bunk in the study.

"Shall I make some supper for them?"

"No, the kids can eat some dry cereal and Jim can share whatever you've made for us."

"Will that be OK?"

"For tonight I think yes. I'll see you later. Bye. I love you."

As he was returning to Jim, he saw the doctor approaching and stopping him asked if it was OK to go up and see Mrs. Porter now.

"No," replied the doctor. "Unfortunately she just passed away. Her injuries were so severe that her heart gave out and her vital organs just shut down."

"Oh my God! I think you had better come over and tell Jim."

"Is there someone who can stay with him? He shouldn't be left alone."

Then Skip indicated he was taking Jim home to stay with him and his wife.

Walking over to Jim the doctor repeated what he told Skip. Once again Jim burst into tears. Doctor Brenner, seeing the state Jim was in, offered to give Jim something to calm him down.

"No, Doctor. We have to go to the police station to pick up his three small children who were also in her car, so it's the best that he be in a position to comfort the children."

"Oh! I'm sorry. I didn't know. Are they alright?"

"Apparently so. The medics that brought in Mrs. Porter checked them over."

"Wait here. I'll be right back." Returning, the doctor handed Skip a box and said, "Have him take a couple of these as I've prescribed. They'll get him through the night."

"Thank you, Doctor." Then taking Jim by the arm, he said, "Let's go pick up the children. There is nothing more we can do here."

***

When they arrived the children were sitting on a desk and were surrounded by several police personnel. They seemed to be in good condition and were drinking milk and eating crackers. When they saw Jim come in, they jumped down and ran to him. Looking behind him, they looked for their mother. Not seeing her, they asked, "Where's Momma?"

A police matron came over and said to Jim and Skip, "They seem to be OK, but they've been asking for their mother. How is she?"

Skip shook his head and said, "She didn't make it."

"Oh, I am so sorry."

Then Skip said, "What do we need to take them out of here?"

"The sergeant has a form that the father has to fill out and sign. Then you all can leave. Where will the children stay tonight?"

"They are all coming home with me to stay with us and my wife will feed them and take care of them."

"That's good because that poor man is in no condition to take care of them. God go with all of you."

Taking Jim over to the desk sergeant, they filled out and signed the necessary release forms and left.

CHAPTER 22

JIM WAS STILL BROODING over the loss of Mary, so Skip helped him complete all the funeral arrangements. Rather than have a viewing with a closed casket, Jim opted to have her cremated to be followed by a memorial service instead. He figured this would be easier to explain to the children that Mommy had gone to heaven. It was a simple service attended only by a few of Jim's friends and several employees of the company.

Since he was in no condition to take care of the children during the day, it was decided that they should stay with Moira until Jim could secure a nanny. Jim could drop them off in the morning and pick them up at night after supper. Moira agreed she would wash, dress, feed, and take care of them during the day. On the weekend they would stay with Jim.

Jim was unsuccessful in his attempts to secure a nanny. It seemed like for one reason or another he thought none of them seemed right for his children. Meanwhile Skip noticed a remarkable change that had come over Moira. She was a completely different person. He was pleased with what he saw. Several evenings when Jim came to pick up the children, he stayed for supper. The fact that he was near and played with the children made Skip feel like an uncle. To say the least, the house radiated with happiness.

But Jim was morose and couldn't seem to shake himself out of his depression. He also seemed to be drinking a little more than he should. Skip wasn't too happy about this but figured he needed more time to make a recovery. As a true friend, Skip suggested that perhaps counseling could help him get over his despondency and indicated the company would pick up the cost. Jim didn't feel he had a problem, but felt he just needed more time so he refused to accept the offer.

***

Back at the plant business had increased so much that Skip had given his approval to purchase the new machine and the project was moving right along. Liz had enlisted the assistance of Frank Kraemer, one of Jim's senior engineers, and Jess to help her with the specifications and review the proposals. Frank had proven a godsend. Although Jim was coming to work daily, he really wasn't doing much and left everything to Frank. Like many drinkers, whatever he was drinking was well hidden and he chewed gum constantly to eliminate any telltale signs on his breath.

Frank was a very capable engineer. He was fifty-two years old and been practicing for thirty years in many different engineering capacities. A former heavy drinker himself, he had quit cold when he injured a boy riding a bicycle while driving under the influence. Hoping that perhaps with a little more time, Jim would come to his senses and snap out of it; he covered for

Jim. A month had gone by since Mary had passed away and Jim still showed no improvement, if anything it seemed as if he had gotten worse.

Tuesday morning Jim didn't show up for work. This was unusual because he never missed coming in. Figuring that he might have had a bad weekend and was either sleeping it off or would be coming in late, Frank made no attempt to call him. When he still didn't show by 10:00 AM, Frank decided to call his house. Receiving no answer he thought that maybe Jim had had to take the kids to the doctor or some other place and would show up later. He wasn't worried but thought, *he should have at least told me of his plans and that he would be late.*

About 11:00 AM Moira called Skip. "You know Jim didn't drop off the kids this morning and didn't call me. When I called his house, I got no answer. You know if he makes other plans I would appreciate it if he tells me."

Skip answered, "That's strange. He didn't say anything to me about any plans. Let me call him and I'll call you right back."

Dialing Jim's extension and receiving no answer, he then dialed Frank and asked, "Is Jim there?"

"No, Skip. He hasn't shown up yet. I called his home but got no answer."

"Gee, that is strange. Did he tell you that he would be late or that he wasn't coming in?"

"No, he usually lets me know if he has something going, but he didn't say anything to me yesterday."

"I think you're right, Frank. Something is wrong. I'll be right down and I want you to go with me to his house. Calling Moira back, Skip said, "Jim hasn't shown up for work and didn't tell anyone he wasn't coming in. Frank and I are leaving now to go to his house and see if everything is OK. I'll call you later."

Arriving at Jim's house, they saw his car in the driveway. Ringing the doorbell and getting no response, they banged on the door which still brought no response, but they could hear voices. Skip now really worried pulled out his cell phone and called the police. When they arrived, he explained that they had rung the bell and banged on the door but got no response and he was worried about Jim.

One of the officers asked, “Does anyone around here have a spare key to get in?”

“I don’t know,” replied Skip.

“Well, let me call a locksmith. I don’t want to go bustin’ down doors.”

When the locksmith arrived, he tried several master keys. When none of these worked, he drilled through the lock cylinder and was able to open the door. Entering, they found the children crying and still in their pajamas.

Skip asked little Tom, “Where’s Papa?”

The little boy, still sobbing, finally muttered, “He’s sleeping.”

Going upstairs to the bedroom, they saw Jim under the covers, ostensibly asleep. When the officer went to try and rouse him, he looked back at Skip and said. “This man is dead. I’ll have to call the coroner.”

“Oh, dear God, no! These poor kids…first the mother and now the father,” muttered Skip.

The officer, turning to Skip asked, “Who is he?”

Then Skip told him he was one of his engineers and then gave him all the particulars and related about the loss of his wife.

“That’s a tough break. Are there any relatives who can take care of these kids?” inquired the officer.

Skip replied, “I don’t know. Jim never mentioned any. I would have to look up our company’s personnel records to find out. They have been staying with us. I’m going to call my wife and have her come and pick up the children.”

***

When Moira arrived, the children still crying ran to her. "Auntie Mo, Papa is upstairs still sleeping."

"Alright. Come with Auntie Mo and let's get you all dressed." After washing and dressing them and taking whatever clothes she thought they would need, she told Skip, "I'm going to take them to the diner to get some food into them and then take them home. These poor children have been through enough."

Before she could leave, the officer stopped her and said, "Ma'am, since you are not a relative, before I can allow you to do that, I must have some identification with your name and address. Then I shall have to report this to the Social Services. They will want to contact you and see that the children are alright."

Giving him the information he wanted, she then took the children and left.

Skip and Frank stayed with the police until the coroner came. After he examined the body he said, "Looks like he's been dead for some time. Do you know if he was on any kind of drugs or medications?"

Skip replied, "Not that I know of."

"Well, the autopsy will tell us." Then turning to the officer he said, "I'll make arrangements to have the body removed and then you can seal up the place."

The coroner left and after Jim's body was removed, Skip had the locksmith put in a new lock. The police then sealed up the house and they all left. Needless to say that Skip and Frank were so stricken with remorse that the ride back to the plant was a very quiet one.

***

Once again it befell upon Skip to make the arrangements for Jim's funeral. As it turned out, Jim had been an only child and also the relatives he had were not close and in no position to take the children or handle the situation. The coroner indicated that while the autopsy was still not completed, the preliminary examination revealed that Jim had suffered a stroke and a massive heart attack and that no emergency treatment could have saved him. Like Mary, Jim was cremated and the memorial service for him was attended by his relatives, a few friends, and vendor reps, and many company employees. His ashes were later interred in a plot alongside Mary's. As a final gesture Skip ordered a beautiful headstone to mark their graves.

His thoughts turned to the children and what was to become of these poor souls now that they had lost both parents.

The social worker, when she came, had indicated that none of Jim's relatives were in a position to or wanted to take the children. Seeing them in their new surroundings, she evidently was quite pleased with what she saw. Skip then asked the social worker what would happen to the children. She didn't readily know, but that usually they would be taken away and put into an orphanage until a relative took them or there was a request to adopt them. Chances were that being so young, they might probably be adopted singly. This was very disturbing news to Skip. He asked was it possible that they could stay in the Well's household a little longer. She indicated this was highly unusual but felt that under the circumstances, something could probably be arranged. She would ask back at the agency.

After she left, Skip, thinking about the remarkable change he had observed in Moira and how fond they both had become of the children, said "I don't know about you, but I can't see these kids being dragged off to an orphanage and then may be split up. What do you think of the idea of us adopting them?"

If he thought she might voice some objection, he was clearly mistaken and was taken back by her response. "Oh you wonderful man! How could I ever have been so blind not to see the goodness in you. I have come to love these children as if they were my very own and would not be happy to see them taken away and split up. I would have been very disappointed if I had posed the same question to you and you had refused." Then going to him, she embraced him and kissed him tenderly saying, " If I ever had any doubts about loving you, I must have been crazy. I love you. There's no one like you and no one I would ever want." Then she embraced him.

When they finally broke, both happy and with moist eyes, Skip blurted, "Let me go call that woman and see what arrangements we have to make."

Though this was a tragic episode, hopefully at least, the ending might be a happy one.

CHAPTER 23

THREE WEEKS AFTER JIM Porter's funeral, Frank Kraemer called Elizabeth. "Elizabeth, I have reviewed all the proposals we received for the new laminator and I think we should get together with Jess and Ken to go over the details."

"Alright. I'll call them both and let's meet in the conference room."

When all were present, Frank laid all the proposals and drawings down on the conference table. Then he proceeded to point out and discuss the salient features of each and some of the drawbacks. After he finished discussing each in its turn, he voiced his thoughts and objections.

After a good give and take discussion, Frank noted their important objections and indicated he would work with the vendor to make the modifications necessary. Then the conversation turned to upgrading laminator #1. While the amount of money would be considerably less, the downtime required to complete the modifications would be far more than production could tolerate. Jess indicated they were already juggling time on some of the other production lines to try and somewhat keep pace with their present production load. After listening to Jess, they all agreed that at this time the best course of action was to purchase a new unit.

The next step, of course, was to invite Skip and Glen to join them so that they could discuss the financing necessary. After Skip and Glen were seated, Elizabeth told them about what had been discussed and decided and the only item left was how to pay the $2,211,000.

Skip, turning to Glen said, "What are your thoughts, Glen?"

Glen, looking at the group, proceeded to outline the options available to them. "First we can try to borrow the sum from our parent company. The interest we would have to pay them I think would be relatively modest and technically would remain within the company proper. I also think that since at this time they are not in a strong financial position there may be some reluctance to give us the money." Continuing, he indicated that they could try to get a loan from a bank or lending institution, but that this might be a bit problematical because of the present economic situation.

He also said that they could go public and enlist the services of a good brokerage house that could underwrite either a bond or preferred stock issue for them. They would now assume a long-term debt with annual interest in the neighborhood of about 7% or 8%. This would entail issuing periodic public financial reports regarding the company's health. Lastly, he concluded, they could issue common stock. This was his preference because the dividends on the stock were only paid out of company profits. Most of the proceeds were kept by the company after all fees and brokerage commission were paid. The money was the company's to keep, with no strings attached, to use for whatever purpose they wanted to use it for. He estimated the company's worth at approximately $100 million. Based on that figure, they could conceivably raise about $10 million by issuing one million shares at $10 per share. This would net them about $9.8 million after paying off all fees and commissions. Part of the proceeds could then be used to pay off the notes on the incinerator thus reducing that indebtedness.

Skip liked the idea but said first he would broach the subject with Sir Arthur Clewiston who could then bring it up before the Board of Directors of BEL. Then he said, "I'll give you the go ahead as soon as I have an answer from Sir Arthur."

Returning to his office he had Rose place an overseas call to Sir Arthur Clewiston. When he answered, Skip said, "Hello, Sir Arthur," and then proceeded to tell him that because of the substantial increase in business, they now needed additional equipment to help handle the increased load. As a result, they planned to purchase a new machine to augment their existing equipment. Giving him the price and particulars, he asked if Sir Arthur could bring the matter before the Board of Directors of BEL for their approval. Sir Arthur was pleased to hear about the increase in business and said he would be happy to bring the matter before the Board of Directors. He indicated that he would contact Skip after the Board reached a decision.

***

Back at the Well's household, things were lots happier now. The children had settled down and no longer cried at night. The children took to Aunt Mo like little ducklings take to the mother duck. She in turn embraced them to her bosom and gave them all the love and affection any mother would give to her children. Skip was happy by the change wrought in Moira as a result and was certainly pleased when he came home at night and they, the children, ran to hug and kiss Uncle Skip.

With the help of the social worker, they had filed the necessary papers for adoption and were waiting for a date to appear before a judge who would make it legal. Weekends now took on a new meaning as they took the children to different points of interest – the zoo, the science museum, the aquarium and whatever came up. Everybody was happy. Even at work the employees noticed the change in Skip. The plant was humming along. They had received two big orders, one from Lancaster Aeronautical for flight insulation and the other from Best Foods for food wrap.

And so it was with much apprehension when the call came from the social worker indicating a date had been set before a judge, but also to tell them that two other couples were interested in adopting children and would also be there. Now anxiety reared its head.

"Oh, Skip! What are we going to do? Suppose the judge decides that one of the other couples is more deserving? I'll die if they are taken away from us."

"Now, now, Moira. There's no point in getting wrought over something that may not happen. After all, we would make good parents."

"Yes, but what are we going to do if for some reason the judge rules in favor of one of the other couples?"

"Sweetheart, all we can do is hope for the best. I'm sure the judge will take note that the children have been happy here with us and not wish to displace them again. After all, we make deserving parents and have a lot to offer them, too."

Skip hoped that his words had a calming effect on Moira, though he knew otherwise. All they could do now was to wait and hope. He didn't dare show Moira his anxiety for he, too, had come to love all the children deeply, especially little Tom, and like Moira he was a little concerned that they might be taken away.

CHAPTER 24

IT WAS TUESDAY MORNING and the board meeting was set up for 9:30 AM. Fletcher was already setting out the glasses and crockery on the sideboard. Previously he had brought out bottles of scotch and gin and a bucket filled with cracked ice and bottles of mineral and soda waters. Later he would bring out carafes of hot tea and covered buffet servers filled with sausages, kippers, and poached eggs.

Gradually the board members started to show up…first Peter Fleming, then Richard Woodall and finally the rest of the board members. Each in turn helped himself to the food on the sideboard and then took a seat at the polished mahogany table. When Sir Arthur arrived, he exchanged some pleasantries and a little chitchat and finally called the meeting to order. First, several orders of business were discussed in detail. These had to do with several companies that were part of the BEL family with areas of concern. In one particular case they all agreed it was in BEL's best interest to divest itself of this particular firm for it was not doing well. The outlook for its future was very bleak with little or no chance of improving.

Sir Arthur mentioned that he had received two overtures from two companies that were interested in acquiring American Laminating, Co. One was from an American in the U.S. and the other from a cash rich Chinese company in Singapore. He had not pursued it further because American Laminating was doing so well.

"Well," chirped in Daniel Hauswirth, "if the offers are any good, why don't we up the price and accept the best one? As I see it, the present business climate throughout the world is rather poor, and will be for some time; obviously, most of the companies in our fold will be having a hard time for quite a spell."

"If A.L. is doing so well, why do we want to sell it?" replied Richard Woodall.

"Several reasons," answered Hauswirth. "First we can get a good price now and second because it really does not fit in with the mix of the properties we now own."

The discussion got lively regarding what they should and should not sell and became heated when David Bascom accused Henry Baudoin of being pig-headed and not looking at the big picture. In his opinion they should sell whatever they could to minimize the losses they would assume while the world economic situation remained poor. "Don't you see how the stock markets of most countries are severely depressed?"

"I see," replied Henry, "but this condition will not last forever and meanwhile we may have sold off some good companies that I am sure will come back. You know, when Sir Charles was approached to sell one of our companies, he refused to do so. I think we should follow his example."

In the end it became a stalemate with four directors, namely John Peterson, Paul Hauswirth, David Bascom and Richard Woodall, keeping open to the suggestion of selling if they received good offers. While Robert Keeshin, Peter Fleming, John Boerner and Henry Baudoin were either not sure about selling or felt they should wait a little longer before making any decisions, they stood firm against breaking up BEL.

Finally John Baudoin asked Sir Arthur, "What is your opinion, Arthur?"

Sir Arthur replied, "Based on the present economic picture, I see most of the companies that are part of BEL will have a hard time making a go of it and their losses may be considerable. But I don't think we should panic and start to divest ourselves of any of our properties. In my opinion, all will bounce back as they have done previously during other depressed periods."

After some more discussion, a vote was taken and all agreed to weather the storm a little longer.

Next Sir Arthur brought up the last item on his agenda which was Skip's request for money to buy new machinery. He related that after viewing the quarterly reports he was receiving, the company's performance was outstanding. They had increased sales from twenty million dollars to well over thirty-five million. He attributed the increase to Mr. Well's management skills and his aggressiveness in pursuing business in new areas. In Sir Arthur's opinion, Mr. Wells had been a good choice to replace Mr. Fulham. He then related the alternatives Skip had given him to secure the additional capital they needed to purchase the equipment. He concluded with his thought that the Board should approve a request for BEL to advance the money they needed. He suggested that it be interest free, or at best with a low rate. He also told them that presently American Laminating received two huge new orders, one in the defense industry and the other in the food industry. He concluded with a glowing report on Mr. Wells and had no doubt the loan would be repaid in short order.

After a short discussion, the Board agreed to give American Laminating 3.3 million pounds and authorized Sir Arthur to send a bank draft at his convenience to Mr. Wells. With no further business, the meeting was adjourned.

CHAPTER 25

IT WAS MIDWEEK WHEN the letter came. It was addressed to Mrs. John Wells and was from the Dept. of Welfare and Social Services. It was a notice to appear before Judge Hardin at 10:00AM on Thursday of the following week. It instructed her to come with Mr. Wells and the three children along with any documentation they had pertaining to the children. A cold fear gripped her heart as she thought *Are we going to lose them? Oh dear God, I hope not.* Picking up the phone she dialed Skip. "We have to be in court next Thursday with the children for a hearing. Oh, John! What are we going to do if they take the children from us?"

"Now Moira, take it easy. There's no point in fretting over something that may not happen. After all, we have given the children a good home…I think as good as anyone else would have done and probably better than most."

"Yes, but what if they take them away? You know there's going to be two other couples there. Maybe we should request a postponement."

"No Moira. What good will that do? It will only prolong the end results. Look, I'll tell you what. Take the children out and buy them some new clothes. Pretty dresses and hats for the girls and a nice little suit for Tom."

"Why hats for the girls?"

"Somehow I always think it makes them look cuter; besides shopping will calm you down some."

"No, It won't because I'll be thinking someone else will be getting my children."

"I told you, don't think that way."

"I can't help it. That's the way I feel. Alright, I'll go and do as you suggest. See you tonight. Love you. Bye."

After Moira hung up, Skip thought *She's right. What if they do take the children? We're going to have an empty house again. Gee, I hope not. We've been so happy with the children and the change in Moira has been phenomenal. There is no question but children do make a big difference in the household. They make it a family. In our case, it certainly has made a great difference.*

***

For Moira the week was a nightmare and it seemed that Thursday would never come. But finally it was Thursday morning. She washed Alicia, Elvira, and little Tom and then they all went downstairs to have breakfast. Skip was already there sitting in his accustomed seat when Moira came in with the boxes of cereal, milk, and bananas. This morning it was Fruit Loops for the kids and corn flakes for Skip and Moira. They each had half of a banana. The conversation was very light because Moira was still a bundle of nerves.

As soon as they were all finished, Moira took the children upstairs to dress them. The girls she dressed in new black shiny leather shoes, white stockings, and dark blue taffeta dresses with white collars and short sleeves trimmed with white cuffs. She then put little gray coats with dark buttons on them and finished with straw hats that were ringed with a dark blue band and a small bow in front and two streamers hanging down the back. For little Tom she had bought a pair of black shoes, white knee-high stockings, a pair of dark blue short pants and a long sleeved white shirt which she buttoned on him. This she finished off with a small blue bow tie. Then over the shirt she put a red plaid tartan vest. When she was finished dressing them, they all looked as pretty as a picture and cute enough to hug.

Arriving at the courthouse they met Mrs. Hammond, the social case worker who sat them down at one table. Opposite to them at another table sat Mr. And Mrs. Robert Martin and Mr. And Mrs. Michael Harper, the other two couples interested in adopting the children. As Skip gazed around the courtroom, he noted it was pretty well filled with a goodly number of spectators.

At precisely 10AM they all rose as Judge Hardin entered the courtroom and took his place on his bench. Turning to the clerk he said, "Julio, what have we here?"

"Case number 684. Your Honor, the placement of three small children for adoption."

"Are any of the plaintiffs represented by legal counsel?"

"No, Your Honor."

"Very well then. Let's get started." Facing the audience he said, "As you know, this is only a hearing and not a trial. We're here to determine the facts and who would be the parents best suited to adopt these children. I will render my ruling after I have heard from all of you. You are free to speak when I direct and give my permission to you." Then looking at his papers said, "Let's start with the Martins." Turning to Mr. Martin he said, "Mr. Martin, will you please stand. Mr. Martin, what do you and Mrs. Martin do for a living?"

Martin, a tall well-built good-looking man with an athletic build, dark hair and eyes stood and said, "Your Honor, I am a vice president and an insurance broker with J.M. Cook. What I do is basically set up company wide insurance plans for large corporations and their employees all over the country. My wife Karen is a part-time therapist with St. Agnes's Medical Center." Karen was also a fairly good-looking blond woman of medium height and build. "When we heard that there might be a little boy up for adoption, we were very much interested. Then when we learned that there was also his sister, we figured we'd take both. Now we see there are three youngsters. We would like to adopt only the little boy and possibly one girl. Hopefully, one of these other couples will take the other child. We will provide a good home for them, Your Honor."

"Mr. Martin, do you travel a lot?"

"Some, Your Honor, mostly in the states."

"I see. Since you both work and sometimes you travel, who will take care of the children while you both are away?"

"We have a built in babysitter, Your Honor. My mother-in-law lives only a block away from us and she would be willing to look over them while Karen is at work, so there would be no problem there."

"Have you or Mrs. Martin ever had to take care of any children before?"

"No, Your Honor. I was an only child and Karen had an older sister."

"Mr. Martin, what makes you think you both are fit to care for children now?"

"Your Honor, it doesn't seem like it takes anything special. You see that they eat, go to school, do their homework and go to bed on time."

"I see. Well, thank you, Mr. Martin." Then turning to the Harpers, he asked, "Mr. Harper, what do you and Mrs. Harper do for a living?"

"Your Honor, I am the regional sales manager for Reaves & Co. We are in the retail business. We sell major appliances and household items," replied Mr. Harper, a short stocky dark haired man in his late twenties. "Mrs. Harper is a teacher in Eastside High and coach for the girls' basketball team there. We would be willing to take the other little girl if she is the only one available."

"Mr. Harper, I also ask you, who will look after the children while you and Mrs. Harper are working?"

"Oh, there would be no problem there, Your Honor. We plan to engage a full time nanny from Germany to look after the child or children whatever the case may be. So there will always be someone home to look after them."

"What experience have both of you had looking after children?"

"I was one of three boys at home and we all looked after each other and Mary has been a babysitter since she was fifteen. So you see, Your Honor, we do have some experience with children."

"I see. Thank you, Mr. Harper." Then turning to face Skip, he said, "And you, Sir, what do you do?"

"Your Honor, I am president of American Laminating Co. Mrs. Wells is a housewife. These three children have been with us since their parents passed away. Their father, Jim Porter, was the chief engineer for my company. We have taken care of them, comforted them, and stilled their cries in the night when they longed for their mother's arms around them to hug and hold them. We have helped them get over the loss of their parents. I realize that both the Martins and Harpers are also good people, but it would be a tragic mistake to split the children up or even take them from us after all they have been through. No, Your Honor, they belong with us. They have come to accept us and love us and now to move into another household I'm sure would leave deep scars in them. Should Your Honor decide to take them from us, you would leave an empty shell in our house and no matter where they go, we will always worry about them. We have come to love them as if they were our own. Even should we lose them and get other children, our thoughts always will be with them. How are they doing, are they happy, are they well? You know the hardest thing for parents to bear, especially mothers is the loss of a child. I plead with you, Your Honor, please don't take these children from us. I promise you this, for as long as I have these two arms and this body, they will never have reason to want for anything. Look at them, Your Honor. Did you ever see three cuter, happier smiling faces? No, Your Honor, this is our family. We love them with all our hearts and they love us. Mrs. Wells and I both live for them; they belong with us."

"Mr. Wells, that was quite an impassioned plea. In the 27 years I have presided in this court and listened to the many cases that appeared before me, there were many times I wished that there were more people like you. I would be totally remiss in my duty to this court if I did not approve your application for adopting these children. You are right. This is your family and my best wishes to you and Mrs. Wells to enjoy them. Then rapping his gavel he said, "Case is closed and this court is adjourned."

The uproar in the court was deafening and soon they were surrounded by many of the spectators who came over out of curiosity to look at the children and wish them well. The Martins and Harpers both plowed their way through the crowd and offered their congratulations.

Mrs. Martin, after seeing the children said, "I am sorry we lost them. You are two lucky people and I wish you all the best of luck."

Mr. Harper was more direct as he shook Skip's hand and said, "That was quite a speech. As soon as you finished, I knew what the judge's ruling would be. The best of luck to all of you."

Mrs. Harper turned to Moira and said, "They are so cute, though we only wanted one, but I think we would have been happy to get all three of these lovely little angels. Our best wishes to you and your little family."

Lastly Mrs. Hammond came by. "Congratulations to both of you. You know I shall have to come by occasionally to see how they're doing. I hope you don't mind."

"Mrs. Hammond, you can come whenever you like either for business or socially, replied Moira."

"Thank you."

Skip looked at Moira and said, "Well, I'm glad that's over. Let's all get out of here and go somewhere where we can enjoy our family."

Moira, embracing Skip said, "I don't know how to thank you. You were marvelous. Yes, let's go."

Taking the children by the hand she said, "Let's all go home." Then they all left hand-in-hand.

CHAPTER 26

THE NEXT DAY FRIDAY was supposed to be a normal day at the plant for Skip. But he wasn't seated at his desk more than five minutes before his phone rang. It was Elizabeth.

"Hi, Skip. May I come up?"

"Sure. I'll be here."

Then Rose knocked on the door and came in. "I know you must have a lot on your mind, but there's a letter for you, Skip," and she handed over a very official looking envelope bearing several foreign stamps. Looking at the envelope, he saw it was from BEL. Opening it, he removed the letter from Sir Arthur. Upon reading it, he exclaimed, "Well, I'll be darned!"

Rose, still standing there said, "Something wrong, Skip?"

"On the contrary. BEL is going to lend us the money we need to buy the new laminator."

"That's wonderful!."

Just then Elizabeth came in, but before Skip could say anything, they both asked, "How did it go yesterday?"

"Moira and I now have three children."

They both exclaimed, "Skip, I am so happy for both of you and the children."

But then Rose asked, "But weren't there some other people there that were interested, also?"

"Yes, there were two other couples, but actually they were only interested in Tom. When they saw the three children all dressed so cutely, one couple said they would take one of the girls, also. The other couple was willing to take either Tom or one of the girls."

"So, what happened?"

"The judge asked us all some questions and allowed us to speak. But after I spoke, the others never had a chance. The judge signed our adoption papers and made Moira and me happy parents. After he rendered his decision, there was bedlam in that courtroom with people clapping and voicing good wishes. Many came over to see the children and wish us well. I tell you, there wasn't anyone in that courtroom that didn't feel something for those three little tykes. Truthfully, the time they have spent with us has made such a change in both of us, especially Moira, that if for some reason they were given over to someone else, our house would never be the same." Then turning to Elizabeth he said, "Liz, BEL has indicated they will lend us the money and has arranged a bank draft with Citibank for 3.3 million pounds which I believe is a bit more than we asked for, so go ahead with the project. Get together with Glen to set up the payment terms and you and Frank go out to the manufacture and arrange the purchase."

By mid-afternoon word had spread throughout the plant that Skip had adopted the children. There wasn't anyone who wasn't happy for both him and Moira.

EPILOGUE

THE AMERICAN LAMINATING CO., under Skip's leadership, doubled in size and became the largest laminating company in that industry. The genius of Bob shined through as he developed many new products for the company to produce. The parent company, British Enterprises Limited, completely satisfied with American Laminating Co.'s performance, decided not to sell it. Dave Fulham, heeding his wife Margaret's advice, concentrated his attention on his own company Atlas Machinery, which became the largest pre-owned machinery company in the U.S. He continued his association with Skip and they became lifelong friends.

The three children: Alicia, Elvira, and Thomas did well in adulthood. Alicia graduated from the Naval Academy and went on to become a doctor in the Navy. Elvira fell in love with her high school sweetheart and a year after graduation they got married and had two girls. Thomas, through his love for baseball, was picked up by the NY Yankees after college and became a star pitcher. Skip and Moira, as they looked back over the years, saw all the happiness the three children brought them and never once regretted adopting them.

And so ends our story. Some stories end in tragedy, some in humor, and some in happiness. This story ends on a happy note. Part of it is based on actual incidents that occurred with the names of individuals changed to protect their identities.

The Author

www.ingramcontent.com/pod-product-compliance
Lightning Source LLC
Chambersburg PA
CBHW020602310726
48979CB00008B/1309/J

* 9 7 8 1 4 2 6 9 2 8 3 3 8 *